HIS

BY

AVERY SCOTT

His First Lady © copyright 2019 Avery Scott

"*You* know that now is when the real work starts?"

Michael Reese rolled his eyes and downed the remainder of his glass of whiskey with a single swallow. It was barely two hours since his party formally announced him as their candidate for President, but his campaign manager, Tom Winterson, didn't seem to be in a party mood. Tom had been lecturing about their to-do list since the minute that Michael walked off the convention stage. This time, Michael moved to refill his glass and pretend that he hadn't heard.

"We can't just sit on our laurels. We have to seize the momentum!"

"I'm sure we can take a couple of days off to relax and enjoy our victory," Michael said dismissively, sinking down onto a large black leather sofa to take the weight off his feet. He paused to take a sip of whiskey and closed his eyes, savoring the brief moment of silence before his campaign manager spoke again. Michael felt like he had been working himself into an early grave these past few weeks. Surely, he deserved a little time off?

Tom didn't think so.

"Tell me you're joking?" Tom tugged off his glasses and dabbed at his balding forehead with a handkerchief as if the very idea had sent him into a panic. "No! We cannot take a few days off to relax. Do you think the Vance Campaign is going to take a few days off to relax?"

"Yes, if they have any sense," Michael muttered. Of course, expecting his opponents to have any sense might be a stretch. These were Walter Vance supporters after all.

Tom perched on the arm of Michael's chair. The look in his eye was one that Michael had come to know and dread.

"You need to get serious if you want to have a chance. Vance has years of foreign policy experience-"

"Does he have five combat tours overseas?"

Tom ignored the comment and kept talking. "He was a two-term governor of Nevada."

"I'm the Senior Congressman from Kentucky and the CEO of a multinational security firm."

"He's got a wife that everyone loves."

Michael didn't have a reply for that. He hoped that Tom would move on but wasn't surprised when the older man transitioned into another one of his favorite topics for nagging. "I think we need to revisit the topic of your love life."

Michael frowned and rubbed his temple. He felt a headache coming on. He wondered if there was any way to head the other man off before the argument picked up steam.

"I'm too busy to have a love life."

"Well, that is something you have to make time for- or at least *pretend* to make time for. It's got to be part of the campaign,"

"What are you talking about?" Michael growled. "The campaign is about my politics!"

"No, Michael, the campaign is about your image," Tom retorted as if he was talking to a particularly dim-witted child. "And the state of your love life, or rather, the current non-existent state of your love life, plays a part in that. People want a President they can relate to, who reminds them of themselves, or at least who they want to be. Mom, baseball and apple pie."

"I have a *mother*."

"But no kids."

"That I know about."

Tom's expression made it clear that possibility of secret lovechildren was *not* funny. He paused to clear his throat before continuing. "You know exactly what I'm talking about. This is the one big area where you can be attacked."

Michael groaned, and dragged a hand through his dark hair. "Tom, I have two ex-wives. I'm a cynical, bitter guy. I think it's best if we just package me as a bachelor and leave it at that. Win or lose, it's who I am."

"How can you be that dismissive after winning the nomination? You have a responsibility to the people who are supporting you. You want to get elected, remember? And besides, the voters won't be satisfied with that. They want a First Lady."

Michael groaned and took another swallow of whiskey. *Not this again.* "Well, I don't have one!" He snapped. "I don't want one, and I certainly don't need one! Now can we please talk about something- *anything*- else?"

IT WAS THREE DAYS LATER, back at Reese Campaign Headquarters in Louisville, Kentucky, before Tom resurrected the topic.

This time, the campaign manager came to the daily staff meeting armed with a newspaper to back up his point about what he had started calling Michael's "woman troubles". Michael didn't have to see the cover to guess what was on the front page. It was a picture that had hounded him during his first Congressional campaign: Michael getting a little too friendly with a young woman that he met at a bar one evening more than a decade earlier. It turned out she was a stripper by the name of Tallulah, and she was more than happy to talk to the tabloids about their so-called "wild night".

"Come on, that's old news! That happened the night before I deployed to Iraq," Michael exclaimed in his defense, exasperated at the necessity of explaining himself again.

Typical. The *one* night that he had relaxed and had some harmless fun was now splashed across the tabloids. The gaffe wasn't even recent. Michael looked around the table, hoping to gain some support from his team. The men appeared amused. The women, however, seemed affronted

"Fine!" Michael glared at his campaign manager. "What do you suggest?"

"I've done some polling," Tom said, and Michael instinctively rolled his eyes. Tom liked polls. He didn't just like them, he lived by them. This tendency had become a point of friction between the men during the campaign. Michael liked to concentrate on getting out and talking to voters directly. He felt polls were a useful tool but didn't put nearly as much stock in them as the other man did.

Tom shot Michael a look as if he were asking for permission to continue.

"Fine, what did your polls tell you?"

"We need a First Lady to keep you out of trouble and to appeal to the electorate."

Michael laughed at Tom's matter-of-fact deliver. "Oh, well why didn't you just say so? That's easy. Let me go into my closet and pick out a wife from the stockpile I've been keeping around for just such an occasion. Or maybe we should just go to the Wife store and buy a new one?" It was meant to be a joke, but once again he sensed the female staffers staring daggers.

Michael groaned. Didn't anyone have a sense of humor anymore? "Fine," he sighed. "Don't keep me in suspense. Who is the next, ex-Mrs. Reese?"

Tom sputtered, seemingly unprepared for the possibility that Michael would ever relent. "Uhm, well I don't know if it will be as easy as that," Tom said thoughtfully. "I mean we would need to vet-"

"Oh, God!" Michael swore. "You mean to tell me you've been going on about this for weeks and you don't even have someone lined up? You pick out my socks for Christsakes!"

"Well, I-" Tom spluttered.

Michael stood up abruptly, indicating that the meeting was finished. Everyone started shuffling papers and reaching for bags. "Never mind, I'll find someone myself," he said to Tom.

"In fact-" a thought had just struck him. He glanced around the room again, looking carefully at his female members of staff.

Kim was too young. Barbara was too old. Laura was too... *pregnant*. Kendall was... Michael paused as his eyes ran over his new speech writer. The tall brunette was sitting at the end of the table, furiously scribbling on a legal pad. Her dumpy jacket and tortoiseshell glasses were trying their hardest but couldn't disguise her curvy figure and pretty face. She was attractive, smart, single, about the right age, and most importantly, *not* pregnant. She was perfect.

Michael caught Tom's eye and then looked meaning-fully at Kendall. Tom silently considered the proposal for a moment, and then shrugged his shoulders. Michael chose to take that as approval. He walked after Kendall as she left the room.

"Miss Bailey!" Michael called after her. She stopped and turned around, flashing a nervous smile.

"Yes, sir? Can I help you? If this is about the speech for the women's institute, I'm almost finished."

"And I'm sure it's going to be wonderful, but this isn't about that," Michael said. He took a step closer and then flashed his smoothest smile.

"It's not?"

"No." Michael paused and considered his angle of attack. How did you ask a girl to pretend to be in love with you? He settled on the direct approach. It'd gotten him far in life so far. "Miss Bailey, how would you like to be my First Lady?"

2

*K*endall was still processing Michael's question more than an hour later when Thomas Winters, Mr. Reese's campaign manager called her into his office to discuss the details of the scheme. She listened to him but only because a part of her was still convinced that he was kidding about the whole idea. What on Earth was he thinking? She was a speechwriter for God's sake, and Michael Reese was a serious candidate. She had only been on the campaign for a few months, poached from one of the unsuccessful candidates for the nomination, but she knew her boss by reputation. One of the things that attracted people to the Reese campaign was his refusal to bend to public opinion when principles were at stake. Somehow, Tom had worn him down, and now he was doing the same to her. No matter how much Kendall protested, Tom had a counterargument. There was no point in debating him. She would have to appeal to Mr. Reese himself.

Back in the coat closet that passed for her office, Kendall tried to concentrate on work, but couldn't find her focus. She squinted at the computer screen but couldn't make any forward progress in her speech. Michael's question kept running through her head. Did she want to be his First Lady? *Of course not*, the rational part of her brain declared. She was a professional speech-writer, and this job was her big break. She had worked hard to earn a spot in a national campaign, and she didn't intend to blow the opportunity by becoming embroiled in a harebrained scheme. Still, she couldn't deny that Michael Reese was a handsome and charismatic man. More than once during their staff meetings she had been distracted by the powerful lines of his body beneath his tailored suits or hypnotized by the bourbon-soaked drawl of his voice. He was practically a rock star to the young voters they were courting. Add to all that the fact that he stood a fair chance of becoming the most powerful man in the world, and you couldn't fault a woman for being intrigued.

Time crawled past. Kendall intended to wait until the end of the day before dropping into Michael's office, but after two fruitless hours of rewriting the same line of text over and over, she decided that she couldn't wait. She checked her hair and makeup before heading down the hall, mentally rehearsing what she intended to say. Surely Michael couldn't be serious? Surely, he understood the risk of undermining his credibility with the electorate? Once she reached the door, she took a deep breath and rapped her knuckles against the smooth wood. She was about to knock a second time when she heard his voice.

"Come in."

Kendall walked in with purpose and was about to launch straight into her argument when she realized that Mr. Reese was on the telephone, so she was forced to wait. Michael waved towards a chair, and then returned his attention to the phone.

Kendall perched on the edge of her seat and tried not to notice the way that Michael kept dragging a hand along his temples, ruffling his salt-and-pepper hair, so it looked as if he had just crawled out of bed. Kendall's toes curled involuntarily at the thought.

Michael finally finished his telephone conversation and turned the full dazzling force of his attention on Kendall. "Miss Bailey," he smiled. "What can I do for you?

Kendall blinked. He knew *exactly* why she was there- unless he and Tom had finally realized that the plan was crazy and called it off? She felt a strange pang of disappointment at the thought instead of relief.

"You *do* remember what you asked me this morning?" she asked warily.

"I think I asked you to be my First Lady?" Michael grinned.

"Yes, you did... and I've been thinking...thinking..." Kendall tried to recall her argument, but the words wouldn't come. She made the mistake of looking into Michael's chocolate-brown eyes, and her mind went blank.

"Yes?" Michael prodded.

"Have you completely lost your mind?" Kendall blurted at last. It was hardly the most eloquent turn of phrase she'd ever come up with, but she was working at a disadvantage. To both her surprise and her annoyance, Michael's grin widened.

"Not yet, Miss Bailey," he laughed. "And I have to say, you're selling yourself short if you think a man has to be crazy to take an interest in you."

"I-that's not what I meant!" Kendall sputtered.

"What did you mean then?"

"That this whole scheme of yours-"

"Actually, it's Tom's scheme," Michael sighed wearily, relaxing back into his chair. "If you have any complaints you should probably take them up with him. I had to agree to find woman to be my fake girlfriend just to get him off my back."

"How flattering for me."

"You're on my team, aren't you?" he asked slowly. "You are working to help us win the election? Doing this would just be another part of your job."

Kendall refused to let him off that easily. "You're going to have to do better than that. I didn't graduate top of my class at Northwestern to be arm candy for some politician."

"*Fake* arm candy," Michael interjected with a wink but settled back in his seat when he realized that humor was the wrong approach. "You're right. You're a talented professional, and this is way outside your job description. On the other hand, Tom is not going to let this idea drop, and I can't risk involving someone that I don't trust."

No wonder he's such a successful politician, Kendall thought, pinking with pleasure at the notion of membership within Michael's circle of trust, even though she knew that he was intentionally flattering her to bend her will. "What makes you think that you can trust me?" She fired back when she regained her composure.

Michael arched his brow, intrigued. "Aren't you one of my biggest supporters?"

"I'm one of your highest-paid supporters."

Michael grinned, but didn't relent with his charm assault. "I see. And since I *know* that English majors are in high demand, I suppose that means I should make this worth your while. I'm asking a huge favor, and it's not fair for me to get something for nothing." He was a businessman and knew how things worked. If you wanted something, you had to give something in return. "What do you want?" he asked thoughtfully.

Kendall looked surprised by this tactic, and it took her several moments to manage a reply.

"What do you mean, what do I want?" she asked suspiciously. "What exactly are you offering?"

"A permanent senior position on my staff?" Michael suggested. "Direct access to the Oval Office when I'm elected."

Kendall raised an eyebrow. "Don't you mean *if* you get elected?" she said dryly.

"I'm an optimist," Michael replied and flashed a devilish grin. "Which is why I choose to believe that you'll come around to my way of thinking." Michael didn't understand why he was pushing so hard for this. He had only consented to get Tom off his back and never intended to follow through, but there was something about Miss Bailey that brought out the competitor in him. It turned into a game the moment she barged into his office and tried to call the whole thing off. He didn't get to play many games these days, so he'd take the fun where he could get it.

Kendall sighed. "For argument's sake, let's say we give this a go. The electorate will never be fooled."

"Of course, they will be," Michael argued, sweeping away her concerns in a single confident sentence. "They'll be fooled because you are the perfect candidate for my First Lady. You're intelligent. You're attractive. You have a way with words. Remember last month when we were at the rally in North Carolina? The teleprompter died, and you came up with the rest of the speech on the fly and fed it to me through my earpiece."

"I only remembered the speech I'd already written," Kendall began, but he cut her off.

"Don't sell yourself short, Miss Bailey. I was impressed. You saved my ass that night."

"Fine, but this is different."

"Well there's only one way to test which one of us is right," he pointed out, no longer surprised to find that he was enjoying himself.

"I still think-" Kendall started to argue but was cut short when the telephone on Michael's desk began to ring again.

"I have to take this," he said, reaching for the receiver.

Kendall stood to leave, but before she made it out of the room, Michael shouted after her.

"Dinner tonight," he said. "It's the least you can do for me since you made me miss lunch."

$\mathcal{M}$ ichael ignored the hemming and hawing coming from the other side of his desk for as long as he could stand. Eventually, after a dramatic sigh, he looked up from the file he'd been pouring over and acknowledged his campaign manager.

"Okay. Spit it out." Michael didn't waste time with words, a trait that he had drilled into himself for dealing with the press. Journalists loved to catch him on the rare occasions that he wandered off message and let his guard down during their questions.

"I can't decide if you should meet Miss Bailey at the restaurant or leave with her from here," Tom wondered out loud, seemingly unfazed by Michael's obvious lack of appetite for the subject.

Michael was growing frustrated. They had at least half a dozen or more important issues to focus on this afternoon if he was ever going to get out of the office and make it on the date at all. This dumb scheme of Tom's was only proving to be a waste of valuable time so far. "Does it really make any difference?"

"Of course, it makes a difference! It makes all the difference. Look at it this way," Tom began, leaning across the dark wood desk as if he were about to tell a secret. "If you are seen leaving together people might talk. You know, it could look a little... unprofessional. On the other hand, if she meets you-"

"I'll pick Miss Bailey up on the way to the restaurant," Michael interrupted sharply. "I have to go home and get changed anyway. Now can we please talk about the crime bill?"

Michael hoped that his expression convinced the other man to move on. He was done with women. Two failed marriages had soured him on the idea of relationships, and he had more important things to do with his time.

Luckily, the firm decision was enough to appease Tom, and they got back to business. Michael was surprised to discover that he was distracted even without Tom's pestering. He kept flashing back to the cute way Kendall's nose wrinkled in shock at the first mention of the plan, and the way she blushed when he mentioned her being his First Lady. The idea of an evening with a pretty, young woman who wasn't afraid to speak her mind was looking more appealing by the moment. He probably shouldn't be looking forward to it quite as much as he was. It was just another part of the job after all. He should keep that in mind.

It was close, but Michael managed to finish getting through the stack of files on his desk and a page-long list of phone calls with just enough time to rush home, take a quick shower, throw on a clean suit and hurry back to the car where his driver waited to whisk him off on his date.

"I told you I'd be back in less than twenty minutes,"

Michael said as Bruno opened the car door for him. He glanced down at his watch and then clapped his chauffeur on the shoulder before climbing into the car. "Nineteen to be exact."

"Everything's a competition for you, Mr. Reese," Bruno teased before closing the door.

Michael was glad when Bruno put the car into drive and navigated the city streets without issue or need for directions. It was embarrassing to admit, but it hadn't crossed his mind to ask where Kendall lived.

The car rolled to a stop in front of a yellow clapboard house with a brick staircase and Chinese Chippendale railings. It was a much nicer neighborhood than Michael expected. Obviously, Kendall had been telling the truth about her status as a high-paid staffer. He got out of the car and walked up the drive to the front door. *Was Kendall expecting flowers*, he thought as he pushed the doorbell. Do people still do that? It was years since his last date. *This isn't really a date,* he reminded himself, struggling to ignore a slightly nervous tingle. This was just a business dinner.

Or possibly not...

Stunning barely described the woman standing on the other side of the door when it opened. Michael almost made the mistake of asking if Kendall was home until he realized a second later that the woman standing in front of him *was* Kendall.

"I wasn't sure what time you were coming," she said, smiling shyly. "Come in. I just need to grab my purse and coat."

Michael stepped into the hall and let his eyes take in the woman in front of him. He couldn't put his finger on exactly how she had changed, but there was something different. Maybe the dress was a little shorter than what he was used to. The black silk hugged her small waist and curved hips in a way her office attire hid. Or maybe her eyes looked a little darker...*smokier*... He cleared his throat, realizing that he hadn't said a word yet.

"You look beautiful," he said, smiling at the way Kendall's cheeks flushed.

"Well, I didn't want to let you down, Mr. Reese."

"*Michael*," he murmured, taking Kendall's arm after helping her into her coat. She looked a little surprised by his familiarity, but Michael pretended to mistake the look in her eyes. "I think we're liable to draw suspicions if you continue to 'Mr. Reese' me."

Kendall smiled. He had a point "All right... Michael," she nodded, testing the name out on her tongue. "So where are we going?"

Michael led her towards the car. He gave Bruno the name of an exclusive restaurant in Old Louisville. Kendall had never been there but knew of it by reputation.

"Will that be okay?" Michael said, obviously pleased by the appreciative murmur that Kendall made when she heard where they were going.

"Very okay," Kendall laughed, "But... don't you think it's a little... excessive? I mean, when you consider that this is just a business dinner?"

Michael frowned. "It's hardly your typical business dinner. Our relationship needs to look believable, or else no one is going to be fooled."

Kendall nodded, wishing she hadn't brought it up at all. She just had to sit back and relax. The most eligible man in America wanted to wine and dine her. What was so hard about that?

"I guess I'm still trying to wrap my brain around this whole thing," she confessed, casting Michael an uncertain little smile that softened his own expression. When he smiled back at her his eyes crinkled at the corners.

"There's nothing to be nervous about," he assured her, reaching to take hold of her hand. Kendall tingled all over when Michael's fingers touched her skin. "We're just two people going out to dinner, but I do understand that this is a lot to take in."

Kendall couldn't help but be amused by Michael's description of himself. "I hate to remind you, but you are possibly going to be the next President of the United States," she said wryly. "I don't think that allows you to be just another person going out to dinner."

Michael made a face. "This is a good restaurant. We won't be bothered too much."

"No?" Kendall looked suspicious. "But isn't that the whole point? For people to notice you and see us together?"

"Well yes, but I thought we could start off slow and get to know each other a bit better."

"And work out the dynamics of our 'relationship'?" Kendall asked dryly. She immediately wished she hadn't sounded so flippant. It wouldn't be hard for Mr. Reese to find another woman to play this game with. As awkward as it was, she had to ask herself, did she really want to give up her role? This could be the chance of a lifetime if she played her cards right.

"You're terribly cynical. Has anyone ever told you that? Somehow, I don't feel like you're completely on board with this plan." He leaned a little closer, and Kendall sucked in a breath. "How could I convince you?"

He already had an idea in mind when he posed the

question. How would Kendall respond to a kiss? She would probably slap his face, but it was awfully tempting to think about. The speechwriter didn't exactly seem enamored with the whole plot of pretending to be his girlfriend, but that didn't mean her lush, painted lips weren't still a strong temptation.

Michael knew that he would have to appeal to Kendall's sense of reason before he took any liberties. He was a politician. He was good at persuading people that he was right. It was his job. He just had to find the right angle, and everyone had an angle if you paid attention. Michael sat back in his seat, a slow smile tugging at his lips.

"Kendall, let me ask you something. Is there any reason why we shouldn't go out to dinner? I mean, since when is having a meal and getting to know someone a crime?"

Kendall stopped looking out of the window at the sound of her given name on his lips. It was warm and casual as if they were friends who had known each other for ages. "Well, no."

"And if people happen to mistake us for a couple, well, that's their own fault for making assumptions," he pointed out smoothly.

Kendall's lips twitched at the corners. "Like in speech writing you mean, when you might use, oh, say an artful phrasing of the truth?"

Michael grinned. "Precisely."

"All right," Kendall laughed. "You win!"

"I always win," Michael said with a playful wink and then looked out the window when the car pulled to a complete stop. "Looks like we're here. I hope you like it. Their head chef is amazing."

"I'm sure I'll love it," Kendall replied automatically as she took in the scene outside the car. For some reason she had assumed flashbulbs would greet them, but no one on the street paid them any mind. She slipped her hand in the crook of Michael's arm and let him lead her inside. The restaurant was dimly lit with lots of dark wood and white linen covered tables. A massive chandelier was the focal point of the high, coffered ceiling. Kendall barely had time to take in her grand surroundings before the *maitre d'* scurried forward.

"Mr. Reese! I have your usual table waiting for you and your guest."

"Thank you, Winston," Michael said, and they were shown to a private table at the side of the elegant dining room.

"Do you come here often?" Kendall asked after the *maitre d'* left them alone to look over their menus.

"Not as often as I'd like. The campaign doesn't leave me with a lot of free time. Besides, it's not a lot of fun to eat out on your own."

A waiter dressed in a black button-down shirt, black pants, and black shoes appeared from nowhere to fill their water glasses and offer a bottle of wine from their private stock.

"Surely you could find someone to come out and eat with you, Mr. Ree- I mean, Michael? Most women would jump at the chance for an evening like this."

"Finding someone to dine with isn't the problem. It's finding someone I *want* to dine with that's a little harder," Michael muttered truthfully. Then remembering himself, he shot Kendall one of his most charming smiles. "Until now that is. We'll definitely have to do this again."

"We haven't even done it once yet! Besides, you might

not like my company. And I caught that, you don't have to pretend to charm me. It's okay if you don't really want to be here."

Michael studied Kendall across the table and sensed that there was more meaning hiding behind those words than what they obviously expressed. "I'm sorry. That's not it." He reached across the table for her hand and gave it a reassuring squeeze. "I've thrown quite a lot at you today. I think you're handling everything wonderfully. It's just a job, after all."

Right, just a job. It bothered Kendall the way he said it, and she had to remind herself not to get too caught up in all the fictitious romance. This was just the start, a candlelit dinner and if she couldn't keep the lines from blurring this early in the game, they'd never be able to pull this off successfully. Kendall couldn't let herself forget that.

Fortunately, she didn't have much time to dwell on her worries because the waiter returned for their orders, and she hadn't even looked at the menu yet. She didn't choose the most expensive thing, although she was sorely tempted. What was the point of going out to dinner with the man who might be the next President if you didn't at least eat well? If there were going to be perks that came along with pretending to be his girlfriend, then she might as well reap the benefits and enjoy some of the finer things in life.

"So..." Michael, leaned back in his chair after they had ordered and were once again left alone. "How did we meet?"

Kendall frowned. She was a little puzzled at the question. "Well, I started working for you. I was originally on the Marley campaign, but when she conceded, I was contacted by- "

"No. I mean, how did we meet? When was our first date?"

"Why can't this be our first date?" Kendall was genuinely confused.

"Tom thinks it would be best if you and I have been seeing each other for a little longer than-,"he glanced at his watch,"-forty minutes...So, we met at a fundraiser? For...underprivileged kids?"

"Oh, because no one's going to see through that!"

Michael continued as if he hadn't heard her. "Your date stood you up-"

"Wait! My date stood me up?"

"Right, that's what I said," Michael grinned. "Your date stood you up, so I very dashingly stepped in and asked you to dance."

"Why can't we just say it happened gradually as we were working together? That really would be the most plausible story."

"You have no sense of romance!"

Kendall rolled her eyes. "Yes. Your staff meetings are so romantic, Mr. Reese."

"*Michael,*" he corrected, "and I'll have you know that I can be very romantic when I choose to be. Just ask my ex-wives."

"Well, the very fact that they are your ex-wives-"

"-Only goes to prove that I wasn't choosing to be romantic enough at the time I was married to them."

Kendall shook her head again, but she didn't feel like she knew him nearly well enough to joke about something so personal and fell silent. Fortunately, the waiter chose that moment to arrive with their appetizers.

Kendall's eyelids fluttered shut, and she made a soft appreciative sound as she took the first bite, letting the delicious flavors burst to life on her tongue.

"That good, eh?" Michael chuckled, causing Kendall's eyes to snap open. A blush crept over her cheeks when she noticed how closely he was watching.

"Why don't you try yours and see?"

Because watching you eat is infinitely more fun, Michael thought but didn't speak. He took an obedient bite of his own meal to appease her, but a wicked thought flickered through his mind. He wondered if Kendall was as responsive and sensual in all areas of her life.

Kendall was more guarded about the enticing little sounds she made as they finished off their starters. She did poke the tip of her tongue out to lick away a dribble of sauce that had missed her mouth and was sitting in the center of the plump curve of her bottom lip. Michael saw it and felt a quickening in his gut that was hard to ignore.

Most of the time he didn't even think about the many months that had passed since he'd brought a woman into his bed. The campaign had taken up every minute of every day and the better part of his nights too. He didn't have the time to invest in a new relationship. *Hell,* he hadn't even had the time to save his last marriage. One-night stands weren't something he was categorically against. He had indulged in one too many to take a pious stance now, but they were too risky for a man in his position and usually not even memorable enough to warrant taking a chance. Besides, he was supposed to be with Kendall now. Tom had made it very clear that other women were strictly off limits. That left Michael in something of a fix. He had just discovered an itch that he wasn't allowed to scratch.

"Mmm, that was delicious." Kendall let out a satisfied sigh. She pushed her plate away and patted the edge of her mouth with her napkin. It caught her by surprise when Michael suddenly reached across the table and brushed his thumb across her bottom lip. The gesture was familiar, not the awkward touch of a stranger.

"You missed a spot," he said innocently. The silky softness of her skin sent sparks sizzling through Michael's blood. He watched as she lifted a distracted finger to touch her mouth. *Interesting*.

"There's something different about you tonight, Kendall," he mused, trying to reconcile the sexy, sultry goddess sitting across the table from him with the no-nonsense, hard-working woman he knew from the office. He liked both sides of her so far and found himself wanting to know more.

"Oh really? It's probably the clothes and the contacts," she fluttered her eyelashes playfully.

"You really shouldn't hide such beautiful green eyes behind those glasses you wear at work," Michael suggested, and then he kicked himself for sounding like he had just stepped out of some cheesy romantic-comedy. He was so out of practice.

"My glasses are part of who I am at work, and I like them," Kendall said in exactly the no-nonsense tone of voice that Michael was used to hearing from her. He couldn't help but smile.

"What?" Kendall frowned, but Michael was saved from thinking up an answer when the waiter returned to take away their plates and bring over their main course.

"Did we decide if we met at work, or at a charity fundraiser?" he asked, cutting into his steak.

"Michael!"

"Okay, okay. I'll move on to something else...How long had you secretly been fantasizing about me before we finally got together?"

Kendall choked. "Excuse me?" she gasped once she had washed down the bit of food with a gulp of wine.

"When did you first realize that you were attracted to me? What is it about me that you love?"

"Your modesty?"

"I was thinking more along the lines of the impressive size of my-"

"*Ego!*" Kendall interrupted sharply. She was smiling though.

"You're no fun."

"Not yet," Kendall let the comment slip, getting caught up in the friendly banter. She hadn't realized the implications of what she'd said until she saw the shocked smile on Michael's face.

"*Yet?* Alright then, now we're getting somewhere." Michael took a sip of wine and then got back on track. "I think I must have fallen for you when I realized that you're as sexy as you are smart."

Kendall blushed. *He was only messing around*, she told herself, but there was no denying the heady rush she felt hearing those words. *What woman doesn't want to be seen that way?* She had never experienced this side of Michael Reese before. Then again, why would she? He was known among the voters for his charm and charisma, but their only previous contact was during strictly professional encounters like staff meetings when he was serious and focused. "Well?" Michael said after a beat of silence. "Aren't you going to return the compliment?"

"Oh, of course!" Kendall spoke quickly. "Let's see, what is it that I love about you?" She tilted her head thoughtfully to one side and pretended to give the question some serious thought.

"I'm told I have a whole list of lovable attributes. Surely you can pick one."

"Your money," Kendall quipped back.

"I'm wounded, Miss Bailey!"

"*Kendall*," she reminded.

"Kendall."

"You were asking for that one," Kendall said before popping another bite of perfectly prepared Chilean sea bass into her mouth.

"Fair enough."

Kendall liked the fact that Michael didn't take himself too seriously outside of the office. He was always focused and intense in staff meetings. It was refreshing to see this other side of him.

"We will need a proper reason though," he said, not letting it go. Surely, he wasn't feeling self-conscious and just looking for a compliment?

"I can come up with a real reason," Kendall promised and tapped her fork quietly on the edge of her plate until inspiration struck. "Ah, I got it! I think... I think I'll say the first thing that attracted me to you was your passion." Truth be told, Kendall was registered to vote for the opposing party, but she had a craftsman's appreciation for Michael's stage presence and the way he worked a crowd. It was impossible to listen to him without feeling how deeply he cared about the issues he was campaigning on.

"Passion? I like the sound of that."

"Not *that* kind of passion! You didn't let me finish." Kendall hurried to correct him, but it was too late. Her mind was already wandering down the dark path of thinking about whether his drive and vigor might transfer to the bedroom.

"Well, I like to think I do more than hold my own in that area of our relationship too." Michael teased. "While we're on the topic, tell me, what kind of lover am I, Kendall?" His voice dropped an octave as he continued, "Do I please you in bed?"

A mental image of Michael, naked and aroused, flashed in her mind. She had never seen him in shirt-sleeves, much less his bare torso, but imagined from the way he filled out a suit that it was all hard lines and firm skin. "I can't imagine when we would ever be asked about that," Kendall choked, growing more flustered by the second.

"Consider it my own perverse curiosity?" Kendall glared at Michael. He didn't think he was going to get an answer much less the one he was looking for. "Come on, you can't blame a man for asking."

"I most certainly can."

"But now I'm intrigued. I want to know what turns you on..."

"Michael!" Kendall scolded him in a hushed tone. She didn't want to draw attention to their conversation. Their corner table was private, but not that private. Besides, she was certain that he was making fun of her. She could see the twinkle of amusement in his eyes. What if he wasn't playing around though? Was that even a possibility? What would she do if he wasn't?

"Finish your steak," she said, putting an end to both her conflicting thoughts and the line of conversation all at once. A woman needed to be on her guard when Michael Reese was in this kind of mood.

"All right, all right. I'll be good," Michael said. "I

guess I'll have to use my own imagination if you won't tell me."

The rest of dinner went much the same way. Kendall was determined to keep up with the witty banter that played back and forth. It wasn't as difficult as she anticipated. She was glad that she had a bottle of wine to keep her relaxed. Michael didn't drink very much, so she consumed at least three-quarters of the bottle on her own.

"How well can you hold your alcohol?" Michael asked, just after signaling for the bill. He frowned, shaking the bottle and discovering that it was empty.

"Perfectly well. Thanks. It's just wine." Kendall wasn't sure whether she had just been insulted. "Why?"

Michael shrugged his shoulders. "It seems like the kind of thing your boyfriend should know. That raises an interesting question though, am I your boyfriend or your fiancé?"

Kendall rolled her eyes. "Haven't we talked about this enough for one night?"

Michael was prevented from answering by the waiter's return.

After Michael settled the bill, he and Kendall got to their feet. "If you're only my girlfriend that will save me the cost of an engagement ring."

Kendall would have liked to come back at him with some sort of sassy answer, but she was using all her powers of concentration just to stay steady on her feet. In hindsight, perhaps she'd had one glass too many. Michael's steadying arm around her waist was nice, even if she couldn't remember him putting it there.

"You looked a little wobbly," Michael said as if he had read her mind.

"Thank you for dinner," Kendall murmured, leaning

into Michael's body a little more. She was pleasantly surprised by the hard physique that met her touch.

"You were in the Army, weren't you?" she blurted without thinking.

Michael stared down at her curiously and considered his words. He didn't like to talk about his time in the military. He was proud of his service, but there were things that he tried to forget. "I did twenty years," he said slowly, "Why?"

It looked like he was trying to work out what had prompted that question and Kendall didn't want to confess that it had anything to do with the powerful, toned body that she could feel rippling beside her. Quick on her feet, she asked, "What was it like? What did you do? I think that's something I should be familiar with as your girlfriend."

"Well...I deployed twice to Iraq before-" he stopped speaking when they stepped outside and were met by a couple of reporters.

Michael didn't nodded hello and stopped briefly for a photo before one of his bodyguards appeared and hurried both him and Kendall into their car.

He didn't look pleased when they were settled inside on the leather seats. "I wonder who tipped them off?"

"You mean it wasn't you?"

"No, of course not. Someone in the restaurant must have posted it online."

Kendall licked her lips and pushed a strand of loose hair behind her ear. She tried very hard to focus. "But I thought you wanted people to know that we're- well-" she waved her hand around "-I mean we're not really, but you want them to think that we're a couple?"

"Yes, but not-" Michael scowled and dragged a hand

through his hair. He was silent for a long moment. When he spoke again, his expression was neutral. "Well, it will probably be fine," he said calmly. "We'll just have to wait and see."

Kendall rubbed a hand over her forehead. "I don't understand why it would be a problem." She struggled to get her head around what had happened and why Michael was upset. He gave her knee a friendly pat.

"Well, it might not."

Kendall didn't have the energy to try and work out what Michael kept hinting at. She would just have to figure things out tomorrow when the world had stopped spinning.

The rest of the drive went by in silence. Kendall slowly sobered up, realization dawning as the haze in her mind began to fade. Was Michael worried that the photographers had snapped her looking drunk? She cringed and sank down further into her seat.

It was true that Michael had his picture taken in one or two compromising positions before, but never with a woman who he had plans on forming a long-term relationship with.

They continued the ride in silence for a few more minutes until the car rolled to a stop outside Kendall's house.

"Let me walk you to the door," Michael said, stepping onto the pavement and offering her his hand.

"Thank you." They walked up the sidewalk together, arm in arm. Kendall unlocked the door but paused before swinging it open. She glanced at Michael's face, and then down at her own feet. It was strange just how real this was starting to feel.

"Did you want to come inside?" she asked without thinking.

"I don't know how that would play out for the voters."

"Oh! I didn't mean-" Kendall blurted, but before she could say another word Michael's lips captured her mouth, sealing inside the rest of her protest.

Kendall swayed in his arms, causing him to pull her tight against his chest. His embrace was the only thing keeping her legs from buckling, as he moved his mouth over her skin, gently rubbing their lips together. She shivered, slowly melting into Michael's embrace as his tongue flicked against the seam of her lips. It seemed to last forever- and, at the same time, not nearly long enough. She couldn't breathe when he pulled away.

Kendall shot a shy glance to Michael's face and was surprised to see that he was smiling.

"Now that," he rasped hoarsely, "The voters will love."

4

The kiss' was all Kendall could think about as she shrugged off her clothes and crawled into bed. Her head was still fuzzy from the wine, and her brain was jammed on a permanent loop- repeating the moment when Michael bent down and claimed her lips over and over again in her head.

Kendall cuddled her pillow tightly while her toes curled against the crisp sheets. Maybe the experience was colored by alcohol and an overactive imagination, but she was sure that it had been one of the best kisses of her life.

Her dreams played along the same lines as her memories, but they didn't stop at the front door. In Kendall's imagination, Michael followed her inside kissing her, touching her, caressing her... She tried to lead him upstairs to the bedroom, but he was too impatient to walk that far. He took her against the wall in the entrance hall, tearing at her clothes, ripping away her underwear and then sinking into her flesh.

Kendall woke with a start, slightly disoriented and

extremely unsatisfied. It took a moment to calm her racing heart. She was just about to snuggle back into her blankets when she glanced at the clock on her bedside table and instinctively emitted a shriek.

She had slept through her alarm.

"Oh my God! Oh, God!" Kendall gasped, jumping out of bed so quickly that she almost fell onto the floor.

She didn't have time for a shower. She rushed into the bathroom just long enough to brush her teeth and pile her hair into a messy bun on top of her head before throwing on the first clean dress that she laid her hands on and sprinting to the door.

Kendall was halfway down her street before it occurred to her that reporters might have been waiting for her to emerge. A quick glance in the rear-view mirror confirmed that fear was unfounded, but she knew that she caught a lucky break. Her sense of relief was compounded when she switched on the radio.

"...was seen dining with his speechwriter, Miss Kendall Bailey." Kendall gasped at the sound of her name and almost swerved into a mailbox. "Michael Reese could be our first playboy President, with two failed marriages behind him, and a string of brief relationships with glamorous women, is his speechwriter really going to be the woman to catch his heart?"

Kendall frowned. What was it about being a speechwriter? Why shouldn't Michael fall in love with her? His 'playboy lifestyle,' as the media liked to dub it, was completely overblown. Yes, Michael had a way with women, but that was only natural for a man who was so handsome and charismatic and intelligent and brave and-

"*Stop,*" Kendall said aloud, embarrassed by her

thoughts. She returned her attention to the radio, some-what mollified when the co-host of the radio show fought in her corner.

"Oh, I don't know. Obviously, none of the previous women have been able to keep Mr. Reese's interest. Maybe a woman who can hold up her side of a conversation will be a change for the better."

"Thank you," Kendall said.

"Well, I don't know how Kendall Bailey fares at holding up her side of a 'conversation,' but if today's papers are anything to go by then the lady in question can certainly hold up her side of a kiss..."

"A... what?" Kendall squeaked. There hadn't been any photographers hanging around when Michael kissed her, had there?

Kendall switched off the radio. It was doing nothing for her nerves. Did people really know about the kiss? Kendall felt a headache coming on. Was this good or bad news? Michael wanted people to find out about them, but probably not like this.

Reporters were waiting when Kendall reached campaign headquarters. They shouted questions that blended together into a single jumbled hum. She forced a smile as she parked her car and was relieved when a pair of burly security guards swooped to her side and escorted her inside the building

Her sense of safety didn't last long. "Late night, Kendall?" the receptionist asked, a hint of meanness in her tone that was at odds with the bright smile plastered on her face.

"Putting in some overtime, were you?" That came from Stan in accounting.

"Were you hoping to 'work' from home today?"

Kendall pretended not to hear the teasing comments that followed her down the hall. She held her head high until she reached her office and shut herself inside. "Why did I agree to this?" she moaned, walking to her desk and rooting through the drawers for aspirin.

Well, she had got one very nice kiss out of the deal, at least. Despite everything, Kendall smiled as she touched her fingers to her lips. Then, she pushed Michael out of her mind and got back to work. A few hours passed. Then, she heard a knock at the door.

"Come in?" She didn't look up from her computer screen until she finished typing a sentence.

"Don't let me interrupt."

Kendall was surprised by Michael's voice. "Oh, I didn't realize it was you!"

"Would it have made a difference?" Michael's grin indicated that he already knew the answer. He shut the door behind him and walked over to her desk. "I missed you at the staff meeting."

Kendall flushed. "Yes. I slept through my alarm. I'm so sorry I-"

"So, you were in bed?" Michael asked, his eyes glittering devilishly.

Kendall sighed with exasperation, and Michael's smile widened. He supposed that he should rap her over the knuckles for missing the staff meeting that morning, but in all honesty, he had been half expecting it. He had dropped her off from their date after midnight. He was glad she had made it in at all. Part of him was concerned that Kendall would try to avoid him after the kiss.

"Well, as I said, I'm sorry. It won't happen again."

"You're wearing your glasses," Michael said, ignoring

the apology as he trained his deep brown eyes on her face. Kendall glared at him through the lenses.

"Yes. I'm at work."

"I have to say that I like what you've done with your hair though," he grinned, unable to stop himself from reaching for a strand that had escaped her bun and winding it around his finger.

"Michael!" Kendall slapped his hands away. "Can you please stop behaving so...*strangely*?"

"I'm sorry," he said and composed himself. He stood up and straightened his suit. "I just came to let you know that the papers this morning didn't jeopardize the plan at all."

"Did you think they were going to?"

"I thought someone might of overheard us at dinner. It probably wasn't very smart of us to have some of those discussions in public areas."

"That's what you were worried about?"

Michael frowned. "Of course, what else could it be?"

Kendall shrugged her shoulders in reply.

"Oh, there is one other thing that I have to tell you before I forget."

"What's that?"

"A few people from the press have asked for an interview. Tom and I have already decided on the newspapers that you're allowed to speak to. He should be along in a minute to prep you. I'm afraid I have to run."

"You're going?" Kendall asked, without meaning to.

"I have an election to win, sweetheart."

"I- of course, you do. I didn't mean... I was just curious as to where you were going," Kendall stammered.

"I'm going to speak to some unemployed auto workers in Detroit, but I'll call tonight."

"You will?"

"I will." He considered dropping a kiss onto her lips but decided not to risk it.

"Goodbye Michael," Kendall said. "And good luck in Detroit!"

ichael left Detroit later than anticipated. He was scarcely able to believe the hopelessness of the families that he met that afternoon. Their factories had been shuttered for months, and the current administration was doing nothing to help. It was heartbreaking. Until he was elected, time was the only thing that Michael had to give them, so he did, remaining at the event hours past the time he was scheduled to fly back to Louisville.

Michael didn't mind the late hours. This was his calling. He wanted to make a difference for people who needed help. He felt guilty when he finally said goodbye and climbed onto his chartered plane.

His late departure meant that he missed a fundraising dinner. Michael was sure that the fat cats throwing the party could muddle on without him, but he did regret the fact that he was traveling back on an empty stomach. He was just trying to decide which fast food restaurant to stop by on his way home when his phone rang. "Hi Tom, checking up on me?"

"I got your message about missing dinner tonight, Michael," Tom said his tone of voice clearly communicated his displeasure. "You want to explain that one to me? It's important to the campaign to get these men on our side."

"Well, I was talking to a few important people over in Detroit," Michael argued mildly. He didn't want to get into this debate with Thomas again. He appreciated that the campaign needed money to survive, but he hated fundraising with a passion. "How are things going where you are anyway?"

"Apart from a few pissed off businessmen? Good. *Great,* actually. The interviews your new girlfriend gave were perfect. I should have left Miss Bailey on her own and gone to Detroit with you. Maybe then you would have come back in time for dinner! "

"So, tell me about these interviews," Michael said, pointedly refusing to apologize for missing dinner. "What did she say?" *What was she wearing?* He thought but kept that question to himself.

"Have you got your laptop?"

"Am I allowed to go anywhere without it?"

"I'll e-mail you the clips."

"Okay, sounds good." Michael talked to Tom for a few more minutes, outlining the next day's schedule before they said goodbye. It was only seconds after they hung up before Michael booted up his laptop.

It took a few minutes for Tom to send the files, but the wait was worth it. Michael's lips curled up in a wolfish smile when Kendall's image flickered onto the screen.

Kendall's look was more polished than it had been that morning, but not as obviously sexy as the night before. She was mesmerizing. He listened, watched, and then winced, as the interviewer asked her a question about his "playboy" reputation. Tom was right though. Kendall had everything under control.

"Michael spends so much of his time working for the country that he just hasn't had time to build a proper relationship with a woman..." she paused and smiled shyly. "Well, until now."

Michael grinned back at the screen, and then caught himself when he noticed the curious stare of a nearby aide. He snapped the lid of his computer shut and resolved not to watch the clips again until he got back home. It was a short flight to Louisville, but not short enough to keep his mind from wandering. Barely five minutes had passed before he began to ponder a truly insane idea.

He wanted to see Kendall. He told her earlier that he would call, but he wasn't sure what the pretense was supposed to be. He thought about asking her to dinner again, but it was too late for that.

Careful, a voice in the back of his head warned him that he was thinking far too often about Miss Bailey. He already knew what could happen if he let himself get carried away.

Michael winced as the image of Kendall was replaced in his mind by the platinum blonde bob and collagen-enhanced pout of his second ex-wife, Blair. While Michael had nothing but good feelings and fond memories for his first wife, whom he married fresh out of college, Blair was an unqualified disaster. Blair was gorgeous, and Blair was fun...*And she could suck a ping-pong ball through a garden-hose*, he thought with a crude leer- but after the first few sex-soaked months of marriage were over, it was easy to tell that Blair had only married him for his money and connections. He was *not* going to make that mistake again.

Half an hour later they touched down at Bowman Field. Michael felt guilty when he saw Bruno waiting with his car at the tarmac. He must have been sitting there for hours.

"Home?" the driver asked as Michael slid into the back seat.

"*Food,*" Michael shot back. Bruno nodded and obediently pulled away, presumably taking them to the nearest drive-thru. Michael leaned back into his seat, intending to catch a quick nap until they got back home, but the scenery outside the window captured his attention. He recognized it from the night before. They were only one right turn away from Kendall's house.

The better half of his mind was screaming at him to remember Blair. Kendall was nearly twenty years his junior and only part of this scheme because she was being paid, but the other voice inside his head- the one that tended to get him in trouble- was craving some fun. He wasn't going to marry Kendall, after all. They were just having a good time. Besides, wouldn't they be more convincing as a couple if they knew each other better?

Well, why not?

Michael smiled as he made his decision.

"Bruno, there's been a change of plans..."

$\mathcal{K}$endall picked up a slice of pineapple, mushroom and bacon pizza, took a bite and perused her notes on Michael's next speech. She sat on the floor in her pajamas, trying to catch up on the work she had to push aside that afternoon when Tom dragged her off to give interviews. She was grateful for the distraction. All the journalists wanted to talk about was her "relationship" with the presidential-hopeful, which was *torture* when she wanted to put him out of her mind.

Kendall didn't do relationships, even fake ones. Relationships were all about feelings, and she tried to suppress those as much as she could. Cynicism is what drew her to work in politics. She could write beautiful speeches in favor of the issue of the day until public opinion shifted. Then, she wrote speeches for the opposite position. She had worked for a half-dozen politicians so far, and all of them had been the same, guided by poll numbers more than principles...all of them *except* Michael Reese.

Kendall glanced up when a car's headlight shone into

the room. *That's odd.* Kendall frowned. She wasn't expecting any visitors. Curious, she put her pizza down and padded to the window. She gasped at what she saw. Michael Reese was getting out of the car that had just turned into her driveway.

Kendall watched in something of a daze as he walked to the front door and rang the bell. She glanced down at her ratty flannel pajama pants and sighed. There wasn't any time to put on proper clothes. At least she hadn't taken her makeup off yet. The bell rang a second time, and Kendall opened the door.

Michael was standing on the front step, wondering if he was going to regret his impulsive visit. He wasn't usually spontaneous, and it wasn't hard to think of a dozen reasons why showing up on his make-believe girlfriend's front porch at this time of night was a terrible idea. Especially when he knew that reporters were lurking nearby. Then, the door opened, and his doubts evaporated.

"Michael?"

He didn't immediately answer. He *couldn't* immediately answer. He was too busy drinking in the sight in front of him. Kendall was wearing a pair of adorably rumpled pajamas. Her glasses were perched on the edge of her nose, and her hair was piled up on top of her head just begging to be tugged free of its elastic.

"I told you I'd be in touch." Michael smiled sheepishly as he awaited Kendall's reaction.

"You said you'd give me a call! I thought you meant on the phone!" Kendall said, and then her eyes narrowed. "You *did* mean on the phone."

Michael shrugged his shoulders, distracted by the fact

that Kendall wasn't wearing a bra. He could just make out the outline of her nipples straining against the thin cotton of her tank top. Once he had noticed, it was difficult to pay attention to anything else.

"I was in the neighborhood. It was easier just to stop by."

Kendall glanced over his shoulder. "Are you alone?" she asked. Michael nodded.

"Can I come in?"

"I guess so, but only for a minute," Kendall said, stepping back to let him pass.

"In here?" Michael asked, heading toward the light on the other side of the short entry hall. The door was open, and the scent of pizza filled the air. Michael's stomach growled loudly.

"Hungry?" Kendall asked. "You stopped by to see if you could beg some food, didn't you?"

"I came to see you, and find out how your day's been," he assured her. "Although, now that you mention it, I haven't eaten since breakfast." He shot her a look that was comically pitiful.

"What was breakfast?"

"A cup of coffee," Michael replied, laying it on thick.

"Okay, okay," Kendall laughed and gestured toward the cardboard box on the coffee table. "Help yourself." She barely finished speaking before Michael grabbed a slice and wolfed it down in a few bites.

"Thanks. I really needed that!"

"No problem. Have another slice. Can I get you a drink?"

No, but I wouldn't mind dessert, he thought, eyeing Kendall's figure again. There was something wickedly arousing about seeing her like this and knowing that this was what she would look like when she crawled into bed. The more he thought about it, the more appeal he found in the idea of crawling in with her.

"Michael?"

"A glass of ice water would be great, thanks," he smiled, doubting that anything short of a full-blown cold shower would cool off his surging libido.

"Are you sure that's all you want?" Kendall asked. "I can get you something stronger if you'd like?"

"Are you trying to get me drunk so that you can take advantage of me?" he asked, letting just a hint of suggestion creep into his voice. Kendall's cheeks flushed, just as he had planned. "I'll just have a glass of water," he grinned, sparing her the embarrassment of a reply.

Kendall nodded and left for the kitchen. Michael stole another piece of pizza while she was gone. He chewed slowly and glanced around the room, genuinely curious about the window into Kendall's life when she was off the clock. The décor was attractive but rather plain. There weren't any pictures of friends or family on the wall. No men, he noted with some satisfaction before he noticed the notes and scraps of paper covering the floor. Michael crouched down and picked one up.

"Don't!" Kendall shrieked, making Michael jump. He dropped the paper instantly. It hadn't occurred to him that they might be important or private, not when they were littered all over the floor like trash

"Sorry," he said quickly. "I didn't mean-"

"Did you move it out of order?" Kendall demanded.

Michael looked over the sea of papers doubtfully. "There's an order?"

"Of course, there is!" Kendall snapped, trying to find the piece of paper that he had moved out of its allotted spot. She was standing close enough to allow Michael to catch a sniff of her perfume. "It's the speech that you are giving at the International Cooperation Coalition next week."

"*Wow*," Michael murmured appreciatively. He had never really given any thought to the speeches that were prepared for him. As far as he knew, someone sat behind a keyboard for a few hours, and a speech would appear. He knew Kendall worked hard, of course, but this showed a different level of dedication. He liked her for her commitment almost as much as he liked her for letting him into her house when she was only wearing her pajamas. *Almost.* "Do you bring work home often?

Kendall shrugged her shoulders, making her breasts bounce. Michael shifted uncomfortably

"Sometimes. I had to today though. I didn't get anything done all afternoon."

"Because of the interviews?"

"Yes, because of the interviews," she sighed, putting the note down on the edge of the couch and temporarily abandoning her efforts to place it back in order.

"And how did you like being in the hot seat? Tom sent me the link to your interview on US This Morning," he smiled. "You looked like you did great."

"Do you think so?" Kendall beamed and sat down beside him. Michael felt his skin prickle from her nearness. "It was strange at first. *Me* being interviewed," she continued, "but Thomas went over everything I needed to say so many times before he let me speak to anyone that I was almost on autopilot by the time they started filming.

"Tom likes to worry about things. It gives his life purpose."

Kendall smiled, and then slowly seemed to realize just how close they were sitting. It made her keenly aware of just how little she was wearing. It didn't escape her attention that Michael couldn't stop stealing glances in her direction.

He was wondering if he had any excuse to kiss her again? Right here and now in her home? He could claim he was only practicing, he could pretend that he was sorry if she slapped him away. Kendall didn't look like she was going to put up very much of a fight though. She was starting to lean towards him, her eyes wide and dark, and her lips slightly parted in a subtle invitation. Michael felt like he was being pulled towards her. It was as if he was caught in a current that he couldn't fight.

He got close enough to feel the shaking puff of her breath as it crossed her lips.

And then his phone rang.

Kendall jumped at the interruption while Michael cursed inwardly. There was no point in pretending it wasn't ringing, so he reached in his pocket and answered brusquely.

"What is it?" he growled.

"Michael?" Tom voice met his ear. "Michael, where are you? I've been calling your home phone for half an hour!"

"Heaven forbid I should decide to go out. I'm surprised you haven't put one of those parental controls on my phone to find me like a child."

"What the hell has got into you?" Tom demanded.

"Nothing," Michael sighed, although he would like to be able to get inside Kendall...

He knew that a kiss wouldn't have satisfied his hunger in the slightest. It would just have been the flame that went on to light his fuse. But bedding Kendall was a bad idea for many reasons. Most of all because none of this was real. He was supposed to pretend that they had the perfect relationship, and whenever he started having sex with a woman, things always started to spiral out of control and hit destruction. He wasn't going to risk his shot at winning this election because a beautiful woman had raised his blood pressure.

"Anyway, what can I do for you, Tom?" Michael sighed, trying to calm his body back down.

"I thought you'd like to know that I've rescheduled dinner with the businessmen you stood up tonight."

"Well. Now I know..." Michael grunted, a second away from hanging up.

"I thought it might be a good idea if you brought Miss Bailey along? She could-"

"Yeah, okay, Tom. We'll talk about it in the morning." Michael said smoothly and then promptly snapped his phone shut and turned his gaze to meet Kendall's raised brow.

"Bad news?"

"Bad timing," Michael muttered under his breath, too quietly for Kendall to hear. "Well, I guess I should probably go," he said, standing up, and holding his coat strategically in front of his body.

He waited to see if Kendall would try to stop him and it was annoying when she didn't. It didn't really matter, he couldn't stay anyway, but she could at least want him to.

"Just so you know, you're probably going to get a call from Tom in a minute to "invite" you to an

47

extremely dull dinner party. I think he wants you to flirt with some businessmen whose money we need," he grunted.

"Oh," Kendall looked surprised. "Why can't you invite me?" she asked, smiling hesitantly and catching him slightly off guard.

It was probably because the blood hadn't fully returned to his brain yet, that's why. He forced himself to smile. "I'm so sorry. Would you care to be my date for a deathly dull dinner party?"

"Well, when you put it like that, how can I refuse?"

"You can't," Michael said, flashing her another bright smile and readying himself to leave.

Kendall smiled again, "I guess I'd better get back to work on your speech, then. Tom will probably corner me first thing in the morning to give his instructions. No drinking, no talking, no flirting-

"Oh, you can flirt," Michael interrupted, following Kendall back towards the front door. "But only with me."

Possessive, she thought. *Very interesting.* "I'm sure that would defeat Thomas's whole purpose of asking me to dinner," she said innocently while opening the front door, and then standing back to let him pass.

"Tom didn't ask you to dinner. I did, remember?" Michael paused in the doorway to look down at her.

"Yes, but only because Thomas told you to. Come on, you can't deny it's true!" Her eyes glittered as she laughed, and Michael enjoyed the warmth of her hand when she patted his arm. "It's okay, I forgive you. I know you're not used to having a girlfriend around."

"I'm beginning to think there might be a very good reason for the that," Michael said in a husky whisper, suddenly overwhelmed with the desire to kiss her again.

He took a step closer and bent forward, only to have Kendall take a quick step back.

"Shouldn't we stand closer to the door?"

Michael blinked, failing to understand.

Kendall repeated her question. "For the reporters, I mean. They won't be able to see us from here."

She walked into the front hall. Dazed and disappointed, Michael followed in her wake. "I'm sorry, if-," he started to speak. He wasn't really sorry, but he didn't know what the hell was going on and couldn't completely dismiss the idea that he had misread Kendall's interest. He wasn't assuaged when she gave his arm a reassuring pat.

"Don't worry," she said quickly. "I know that this is all part of my job. You'll find that we speechwriters are very adaptable."

"Oh?"

"Well, we have a lot of practice, don't we?"

"Kissing co-workers?"

Kendall laughed, "Giving people a show. Telling them what they want to hear. Showing

them what they want to see." She didn't notice the frown that shadowed his features until she turned around.

"Is something wrong?"

"No," Michael said quickly, forcing his lips into a tight smile. He made a cursory glance out the door before turning back to face her. "It looks like the reporters are taking the night off."

"No kiss then?"

Michael stared at her, wondering if she was aware of the mixed signals she was sending. Was she 'telling him what he wanted to hear', or did she feel the same magnetic pull that he did whenever she was near? The temptation to go ahead and kiss her was strong- but he still had his pride.

"Why don't you take the rest of the night off?" he said, ignoring her question and hoping that she missed the bitterness in his tone. "Goodnight, Miss Bailey. I'll see you at work tomorrow...this time, don't be late!"

7

*M*ichael breathed out heavily once he was safely shut inside the car, frustrated and confused, tingling with the sting of rejection and the restless energy of unfulfilled desire. He had never thought that simply being around Kendall would have this kind of effect on him. Every sense seemed heightened in a way that he hadn't felt in a long time. There was no way he was going to get any rest tonight.

The irony of the situation was he couldn't go out and 'scratch the itch' with some other woman because then he'd be cheating on his make-believe girlfriend. Besides, right now he didn't want some other woman, he wanted Kendall. Until a few minutes earlier, he believed that the feeling was mutual. He wasn't immune to the blushing, and he noticed the way she melted into him when he kissed her goodnight yesterday. He had a good idea where a kiss on her couch would have led them.

A kiss for reporters might be "part of the job", but he hoped that a little more time alone could convince her to work a little "overtime". They were two consenting adults after all, so, if he wanted to have sex with her and she wanted to have sex with him, what was the problem, he tried to rationalize. Why couldn't they just give in to what they both wanted?

"Because..." Michael muttered aloud.

Well, because none of this was meant to be real. Kendall was right. This was a job. They had an objective - to get him elected as the next President. If they started muddying the water with feelings, or at least, passions, then things would spiral out of control. He would upset her one way or another and then she would leave, blowing the campaign, and before he knew what was happening, he'd have another scandal on his hands.

It was just a bad idea all around. He wished his body would get on the same page as his mind.

Fortunately, by the time he arrived home, his desire was imperceptible to his housekeeper, but Michael was still vaguely aware of the buzz from unfulfilled lust that was still zipping through his veins.

"Can I get you anything to eat, sir?" Mrs. Martin asked as soon as Michael stepped inside the front door. "I've made a stew and left it in the fridge. Did you want me to heat it up for you?"

Michael smiled and shook his head. He thanked the housekeeper and said goodnight. He walked Mrs. Martin out to her car as he did every night to make sure the aging woman got off safely, carrying any bags she had, and making sure her antique car started.

There was something wonderfully liberating about walking back into his empty house all alone. It was as though he left public (hopefully) soon-to-be President Reese outside, and could go back to being plain old Michael once he was on his own. There was no one watching, waiting for him to slip up, looking for a story, or digging for a scandal. On the flipside, there was no one at all. That could feel lonely at times too, or at the very least frustrating.

He really, *really* needed a woman. That had been one of the positives of having a wife. There was always a steady supply of sex. Well, in the early days at least.

Michael took Mrs. Martins' beef stew out of the fridge and put it into the microwave, shrugging off his suit jacket as he waited for his dinner to heat up. He wondered if Kendall had finished her pizza. He wondered if she was in bed yet and he couldn't shake the thoughts all throughout his dinner.

"Stop it!" he told himself as he got undressed for a quick, hot shower. He took one last glance at his cell phone and frowned when he saw that he'd missed a call. He checked his voicemail, rolling his eyes when he heard Tom's voice. His campaign manager was obsessing over some little detail that could have waited until morning. Didn't the man ever switch off? Michael decided to turn his phone off for the night. He didn't need Tom calling and waking him up in the early morning hours.

After his shower, he dried off quickly and sank into bed. He never slept with clothes on, hating the constricting feeling when he moved around at night. The king size bed felt especially oversized tonight as he stretched his large frame across it, wishing someone soft and warm was lying next to him. It was the last thought he had before immediately falling asleep.

---

8

*K*endall also passed a restless night. Every time she tried to drift off to sleep, images of Michael filled her head. She wasn't sure how she felt about the man who showed up at her house out of the blue tonight. She kept thinking about the look in his eyes when she dodged his kiss. Was she imagining his disappointment? Less than a week earlier, she had never thought of Michael as anything but her boss. Well, that wasn't *completely* true. She had admired his fine physical features a time or two. She was, after all, a human female with a pulse. It was impossible to ignore the fact that the man was *gorgeous,* with a magnetic personality to match. When she first joined the campaign, she knew where she stood and would never have attempted to catch his eye. But now, she didn't know anymore. Michael had picked her out for the 'job' for some reason. That had to mean something, right? He at least found her attractive enough. The flirting, it couldn't all be an act, right?

Kendall thumped her pillow and shifted around, trying to get comfortable. She could admit to herself that she had always found Michael physically attractive and mentally stimulating, but who knew that he could be so funny or so charming?

It was a problem.

This is why I don't do the "boyfriend" thing, Kendall thought with a sigh. She liked men. She liked sex, but she hated the psychological torture that always seemed to be lurking just beneath the fuzzy warmth of new love.

Kendall was seven when her dad walked out. It was the ultimate cliché exit. After a fight with her mom, he went to the store and never came back. Kendall saw him walking out the door.

"Bring me some gummi bears."

That was the last thing she ever said to her father. Those five stupid words were drilled into her head. Why hadn't she told him that she loved him? Why didn't she ask him to stay? Why didn't she promise that her mother would forgive him, or that she could make it better? She couldn't let it go.

A string of "uncles" followed in her father's wake. Rich men. Poor men. Businessmen. Doctors. It didn't take Kendall long to figure out the combinations of words and smiles to earn a new barbie doll or a trip to the beach. She couldn't make any of them stay...but she tried. It was the perfect training for what Michael was asking her to do. She could charm his donors and coo over babies and make everyone think that she was on their side. She wasn't worried about making the public believe that she was in love with Michael, she was afraid of succeeding too much.

Despite everything, Kendall knew that she was going to be in trouble if Michael paid anymore spur-of-the-moment visits late at night. She might not want a relation-ship, but that didn't mean that she could ignore the physical attraction that she felt whenever he was near. What she *should* do was insist that he leave her alone when the cameras were off. What she most likely *would* do was take a little more consideration in what she wore to bed from now on, just in case there were any more surprises. Kendall shivered as she remembered some of the looks that she had caught in Michael's eyes when he was staring at her. It was too bad about the lack of reporters. She really regretted that she blew her chance at a second kiss.

Kendall rolled onto her back and cast her thoughts back to the moment that they had shared the night before. She didn't know if her mind had made it into something it wasn't. The only way to know was to kiss him again. *For research purposes* only, of course. She just wanted to see if her memory was playing tricks on her.

Kendall smiled into her pillow, finally finding a position that was comfortable to sleep in. How did one go about enticing the future President to kiss you? It might be a lot of fun trying to find out.

Kendall's dreams were good enough to let her live out that fantasy in a few different scenarios once she fell asleep. When she finally woke the following morning, she was embarrassed to find herself clutching a pillow against her cheek.

"What are you doing to me, Michael?" she sighed, stretching and glancing at her alarm clock. She wasn't sure what had woken her. She still had half an hour before she needed to get up.

Kendall had just snuggled back under the blankets, trying to pick up with dream Michael where they'd left off, when the doorbell rang. She groaned and threw off the covers when it rang a second time. It seemed this person was not going to go away, but what kind of lunatic came by unannounced at 5:30am?

It couldn't be, could it? Was Michael downstairs behind her front door?

Just because he surprised her last night didn't mean he'd do it again in the morning. It was incredibly unlikely; however, Kendall couldn't stop thinking about the possibility as she reached for her robe and glanced in the mirror at her reflection. She wanted to pull a comb through her hair, but she didn't have time if she wanted the doorbell to stop its incessant ringing.

Kendall hurried downstairs, breathless and rosy-cheeked. She unlocked the front door, threw it open, and couldn't hide the look of disappointment on her face as she identified the visitor.

"Mr. Winterson? What a surprise." Kendall pulled her robe more tightly around her waist and tried to cover her annoyance with a smile. "What are you doing here?"

"I'm sorry to disturb you so very early, Miss Bailey," the plump, balding man said as he eased his way into the foyer uninvited. "However, I thought I should take it upon myself, now that your status has changed somewhat, to see that you have your own chauffeur and car." Tom beamed, pointing over his shoulder to the shiny Mercedes that was sitting in the middle of Kendall's driveway.

"Oh... wow. Seriously?" Kendall said. The perks just kept coming. This was a nice luxury but was it necessary? Especially this early in the morning. "Does er- Mi- Mr. Reese know about this?"

"I'll inform him during our morning briefing. I'm also here to make sure that you're ready for dinner tonight," he said, still smiling.

"Dinner, but it's 5:30 in the morning?" Kendall frowned. "Couldn't this wait until I got in the office?"

"I've been talking to some of our people, Miss Bailey, and well- we're not sure if we've got your image quite right yet," Thomas confessed. "So we'd like you to spend the day with some make-up artists and fashion designers."

"But I- my- speech," Kendall whimpered, looking pitifully towards the living room where all her notes were still waiting for her.

What kind of woman was she that she would rather sit down at her computer and type up a speech for Michael on inner-city poverty than go and be pampered and play dress up, she asked herself. The answer came readily enough. She was a woman who thought substance was more important than style. It was more important to her for Michael to have a speech that sounded strong and convincing than it was for him to have a perfectly polished woman on his arm. Besides, if she gave any more thought to the idea of needing a stylist of any sort, she might just feel a bit offended.

"Mr. Winterson, I really can't-" Kendall tried to argue, but she didn't think that Thomas was listening to her. In fact, he was shooing her back upstairs to get dressed.

9

"What do you mean she's not in her office?" Michael frowned, glaring accusingly at the young temp who was working the reception desk at his campaign office that day. It was lunchtime, and he had come downstairs to ask Kendall if she wanted to grab a bite to eat with him. He was still unsettled by their parting the night before. Was he imagining the attraction between them? He needed to see her again to find out. It was frustrating to find she wasn't in her office.

"As far as I know, Miss Bailey didn't come into work this morning, sir," said the girl. It was obvious from her meek tone that she was nervous about giving a disappointing answer to Michael, considering who he was. "I- I haven't seen her all day."

Michael nodded, realizing he was being a bear when it had absolutely nothing at all to do with this girl. He thanked her for the information and forced a smile before he walked back to his own office. Where was Kendall? Had he pressed things too far?

It didn't take too long to find out. In fact, a telephone

call from Tom told him everything he needed to know when he got back to his office.

"You're doing *what* with her?" he demanded. Tom started in on relaying his crazy plan to create the perfect First Lady. "Look, can you put Kendall on the phone? I think I need to have a word with her."

There was shuffling, rustling and murmured voices before Kendall finally spoke.

"Hello?" Kendall sounded confused. For whatever reason Michael was even more irritated than before when hearing her voice. He hoped that Kendall knew the makeover wasn't his idea. He didn't want to change anything about her. No one was perfect, but so far, she was damn close. Still, it was annoying that she was playing dress up with his campaign manager when Michael needed her at work.

"Miss Bailey," he said, using her last name intentionally. "I went to your office to see you earlier."

"You did?"

He took a sick kind of pleasure in hearing the guilt in her voice. He knew how seriously she took her job. "Obviously you weren't there," Michael continued, keeping his voice crisp and cool. "I thought we could go over the poverty speech while we had lunch together, but Tom informs me that you're busy." He was acting petty and unfair, Michael hated himself like this, but he couldn't stop. He had seen the night before how hard Kendall worked, but that didn't stop him from continuing. "When do you think you might have time to finish off a draft for me to look at?"

Michael heard the hurt catch in Kendall's breath, but he was still feeling out of sorts enough to take a gleam of satisfaction from it.

"I'm not-" she suddenly stopped trying to defend herself and answered Michael in a cool tone to match his own. "I'll have a copy on your desk in the morning, *sir*."

The use of *sir* was not lost on Michael, and it irritated him even more. "Remember, you're still coming to dinner tonight, Kendall." It wasn't a question. It was a statement.

"I'll have it finished," Kendall stated again simply.

"Kendall, listen you don't-" Michael started to soften up but was interrupted before he could finish. He didn't stay angry for very long, but while he was angry, he could be small-minded and cruel.

"I said I would finish it by tomorrow morning," Kendall repeated "It's my job. I'll have it done for you, Mr. Reese. Goodbye," she said, and then she hung up.

Kendall's hands were trembling with fury when she passed Thomas back his cell phone. She had never felt so insulted in her life. Michael had no right to insinuate that she was letting her "real" job slide. She had never missed a deadline. What's more, he had first-hand knowledge of how hard she worked when he stopped by her house the night before. She had thought that Michael had approved her new makeover, and even if he hadn't this wasn't her idea. It was Tom's. At least she could stop worrying that it was Michael who had set it up because he didn't find her appearance to be up to his standard. It was a small consolation, but it didn't make up for the fact that he had been such an asshole on the phone.

Kendall should have trusted her initial instincts that morning. *None of this trivial stuff mattered*, she had thought while looking around her house. Hair products, a rack of designer clothing and makeup were strewn about everywhere she looked. The clutter was driving her nuts, and so were the people that brought them to her house.

Fortunately, they were just about wrapping up, and it would all be gone soon. Once she could scoot them all out of the door, Tom included, she could focus on that speech she'd just promised by tomorrow morning. Kendall thought she might cry. She was only half-way through with the speech, and there wasn't much time to finish things up, especially when she still had to be paraded around for dinner.

"Who needs sleep, anyhow?" Kendall muttered under her breath, mentally resigning herself to another late night. At least the adrenaline of an upcoming deadline would keep her on task. She would probably be further along right now if she hadn't devoted quite so much time to daydreaming about her boss.

By the time evening came Michael had time to reconsider his behavior on the phone and to regret the conversation that he had with Kendall. He wouldn't say that he was apprehensive about seeing her again, he really didn't know what to expect. Any anticipation that he felt about seeing her was tempered with uncertainty over what kind of reception he would receive.

He would simply have to be at his most charming to win her over again before they left for their dinner in Washington, D.C. The limousine would be the perfect first stage for an apology. Michael had made sure there was champagne on ice to help soften Kendall's defenses. He had even brought flowers, although he had no idea which type her favorite were. He opted for the standard red roses, it seemed a safe bet.

When they pulled up outside her house, Michael squared his shoulders, straightened his tie and steeled his resolve. He could be a man about this, he told himself, giving a little pep talk along the way. He would just walk up to the front door, and when she opened it, he would say-

"Wow!"

Of course, Michael had meant to say that he was sorry, but he was too busy trying not to drool down his chin. Kendall looked like she just stepped out of the pages of a magazine, or at least right out of his dreams.

"Kendall you look-"

"Let's just go, shall we?" she said in a sharp business tone, sweeping past Michael and leaving him to watch the hypnotic sway of her pert little behind as she walked.

Damn, she was holding a grudge, and he had somehow forgotten the flowers. The thought managed to burst through a lustful haze that was fogging his brain. The bouquet was still in the limo, but at least Kendall's expression softened slightly when she saw them sitting inside the car. She didn't comment, however. She simply climbed inside and waited for him to follow.

Michael hopped in readily, unable to peel his eyes away from the delectable figure of the woman now sitting beside him. He was just trying to decide how to launch into a neutral topic of conversation when Kendall reached into her purse and took out her iPad.

Michael frowned. "What are you doing?" he demanded. His frown turned into a scowl when Kendall insisted on giving her full attention to her iPad. "Kendall?" It was his turn to be irritated. He knew that losing his temper again wasn't going to help in the slightest, but this woman had the ability to rattle him effortlessly. It probably had something to with the fact that he was still trying to work out a way to get into her panties. He wondered if they were red to match her dress.

"I'm working on your speech, *sir,*" Kendall sniffed,

chewing her bottom lip thoughtfully as she read over her work so far.

Michael was sure the little gesture was made to annoy, not to arouse him, but whatever Kendall's intent was, his body clearly had ideas of its own on how to interpret the sight of her teeth nibbling on the plump swell of her lower lip. He wanted to lean forward, catch it between his own teeth.

"Ugh- why are you working on that now?" Michael asked, shaking his head to try and clear his thoughts.

Kendall looked at him coldly. "Because you told me that you wanted it finished and on your desk tomorrow morning, *sir.*"

Suddenly, Michael smiled. He had a flash of inspiration and determined how he could use her little snit to his advantage. "And do you always intend to do everything that I tell you?" he asked huskily. He could think of one or two instructions that he would love to give Kendall if she was willing to follow them. Unsurprisingly, she wasn't quite ready to forgive him and play along.

She continued to regard him icily. "I did not like the way that you implied I wasn't doing my job this morning!" she told him bluntly. "Mr. Winterson arrived at my house at the break of dawn to drag me out of bed!"

"Tom arrived *when?*" Michael asked incredulously, unable to suppress a flare of jealousy at the thought of another man being with Kendall for so long at her home- and in the same enticing pair of pajamas that he had seen.

Kendall put down her iPad. "He showed up at five-thirty! I was still in bed!"

Still, in bed, Michael shifted in his seat uncomfortably. "I'll have a word with Tom," he murmured, still unsure as to why the man had decided to take this matter into his own hands and not tell Michael what he was doing. Tom often frustrated him with his actions, but this was going a bit across the line.

"Oh, don't worry about it," Kendall sighed, as she returned her attention to her iPad. "I don't see it happening again, so it's not that big a deal."

Michael grunted something and tried not to sulk as she went back to writing his speech. She would have to stop playing around with the thing for at least a while when they arrived at the airport. He would just have to hope that he could focus her attention on him then.

The rest of the short ride to the airfield was boring, Michael sat brooding in silence and let Kendall continue with the speech. Kendall mistook the brooding to mean he was didn't want to interrupt her, and she should carry on diligently. It was starting to piss her off all over again. If he expected her to work tirelessly and to give up every second of her day to help with his campaign, then he had another thing coming. She stared at her iPad, anger at a low boil until the limousine finally came to a halt.

"Are we-" Kendall stopped speaking when she saw where they were. She blinked at Michael. "We're at the airport?"

"We are," he nodded, and then he took her hand and helped her out of the car. "We're flying to D.C.," he informed her, keeping hold of her hand, even as Kendall tried to tug it back.

"D.C.? That's insane! I can't go to D.C. tonight!" she gasped.

Michael couldn't help but smile at her surprise. He took the opportunity of her lowered guard to urge her forwards by placing a hand at the small of her back. It was a sweet yet intimate gesture that he probably should have avoided because it made his pulse jump and his body tingle.

"Tom forgot to inform you of that little detail, did he?" he asked, smugly. "Guess he was too busy playing make-over."

"You could have told me!"

Michael shrugged his shoulders innocently. "I was hoping it would be a surprise," he confessed.

"Well, I can't imagine why!" Kendall didn't sound really upset, however, and once she was settled on the plane, she seemed to enjoy her surroundings. The plane had been rented to ferry him across the country to campaign events. The luxurious surroundings blunted the misery of nearly-constant travel.

Despite her determination to stay angry at Michael, Kendall couldn't help but betray her delight with the novelty of flying on a private plane. The soft black leather seat felt like butter when she sank back into it, and a soft sigh escaped her lips. She had only flown first class a few times in the past. This took things to an entirely new level. She continued to take in the surroundings until Michael's voice interrupted her.

"I was going to offer you a drink earlier, but you didn't seem in the mood. Would you like something now?" There was a hint of amusement to his voice, and Kendall caught a glimpse of his smug smile.

"I'll just have ice water, thank you." She was determined to keep her wits about her this evening.

The flight was pleasant and surprisingly brief. Kendall refused to drink anything stronger than water, but Michael refused to leave her in peace.

At first, Kendall rebuffed Michael's efforts at conversation, but he was quite persistent. One of the many reasons he was good at his job. When it became clear that he wasn't going to give up, she surrendered and put the iPad back in her bag.

"So, it's really important for us to make a favorable impression on these businessmen?" Kendall asked. "Thomas said it was vital for the campaign."

Michael frowned. "Well it would certainly make funding a lot easier," he admitted. "Still, I would rather not have to pander to them. It's not my style in general. Unfortunately, the campaign won't pay for itself."

"Careful, Michael, you're starting to sound like an idealist," Kendall teased. She placed a reassuring hand on his knee. "I know you wouldn't make a deal with anyone completely unprincipled."

"But you would."

Kendall gasped, wondering if she had just been insulted. "I would?"

"Isn't that your specialty? Telling people what they want to hear?"

Kendall didn't know how to respond, and so she remained silent. She followed Michael's eyes to her hand that was still resting warmly on his leg. She was suddenly very much aware of the powerful muscle that had tensed beneath her touch. She knew it was a mistake, but she couldn't seem to pull her hand away. Instead, her pulse quickened, and her breathing became shallow as she lifted her eyes to meet his.

Michael's gaze was hot and inviting, almost daring her to smooth her hand higher up his leg to see what she would find. It was so very tempting. Just as Kendall's fingers flexed, the stewardess ruined the moment by walking over to inform them both that they would be landing soon and asked them to fasten their seatbelts.

Kendall snatched her hand away as her sanity snapped back into place. What on Earth made her do that? It felt so natural at the time, but now she was left with a pit in her stomach. She couldn't bring herself to meet Michael's gaze as they landed in D.C. and disembarked. Michael didn't seem to suffer any similar signs of embarrassment. When he spoke, it was as if nothing at all had happened on the plane.

That was an attribute she admired. Michael was such a good politician that sometimes she couldn't read his true feelings at all. Everything he said and did came across as genuine, whether you liked it or not. In addition to that, from what she could tell, he could brush things off and move on as if they'd never happened.

"The restaurant isn't far," Michael informed Kendall, staring at her pointedly when she began rummaging in her purse. "You're not going to have time to work on that before we get there."

"Work on what?" Kendall asked innocently.

"Kendall, forget about finishing the speech by tomorrow morning, would you? Just enjoy tonight? I was an ass earlier."

Kendall didn't contradict him, but she did sigh heavily. It was as close to an apology as she was probably going to get. Besides, he wasn't wrong to expect her to be at work, but in her mind, she was at work, in a way: Her part-time gig as a girlfriend.

"You were right about it being my job though. I really can't keep taking time off to have my nails done," Kendall muttered.

Michael grinned. "Well if it makes you feel any better, I think your nails look lovely. You can't have a First

Lady who doesn't have pristine nails," he said, keeping a straight face.

Kendall relaxed a bit. "Thanks, it doesn't really help, but I appreciate it anyway," she said. Her eyes traveled to the large gray stone building outside of their car when they pulled up. "Ooh? Is this the place?" she asked, taking in the scene. Fairy lights enchanted the sparse trees outside lending to a romantic feel. At least from the outside, it appeared she was in for an even nicer dinner than the one they shared before.

"This is it," he nodded. "One of the men we're here to see owns this hotel," he told her, helping Kendall out of the car.

"Really? Now you did say that all these guys are single, right?" she teased, taking his arm.

Michael bristled but tried to force a smile before reminding her of their deal. "Just remember that *you're* not single, sweetheart," he whispered, slipping a possessive arm around her waist.

The feel of Michael's body against hers was comforting as they walked together towards the entrance. "I thought I was meant to flirt with these men?" Kendall laughed. "Isn't that's why you brought me along? You know, I can just go back and sit in the car and work on your speech if you don't need me to stay around."

"Ah, but I do need you," Michael said slowly, huskily, trying not to think about all the ways in which he needed her, *wanted her.* Just how was he meant to concentrate on business when all he could think about was getting Kendall on her back? Every time he touched her it got harder and harder not to press the issue. "I'm just rethinking this scheme you and Tom have come up with," he murmured.

"Don't even. This was all you and Tom. If you remember, I wanted nothing to do with it!" Kendall started to argue, but she couldn't continue, because the *maître d'hotel* had just spotted the pair and was hurrying over to greet them.

"Monsieur! Mademoiselle! Monsieur Ramos is expecting you."

Michael and Kendall were led in the direction of a private room, away from the hotel's other clientele. The maitre d' announced their arrival to four very smartly dressed businessmen.

"Michael! Glad you could join us!" An olive-skinned man in an impeccably tailored Italian suit rose to greet them as they walked through the door. "We were disappointed that we missed you in Detroit...but I hear you've been a little busy lately. I suppose this is your lovely distraction?"

Michael placed his hand on the small of Kendall's back and forced himself to smile as he introduced her. He frankly didn't like the look in Ramos' eyes. The other man looked her up and down, his dark eyes conveying their satisfaction with what they saw.

The other three men, two oil tycoons and the head of an international retail company, were less extravagant in their praise of Miss Bailey, but their subtle appreciation didn't go unnoticed.

"Michael, my wife, isn't going to be happy to hear I left her at home with the children when you brought your lovely girlfriend here!" laughed Roberts, one of the two Texas oilmen.

Personally, Michael thought that Mrs. Roberts was going to be more upset if she heard about the way that her husband was trying to look down the front of Kendall's dress.

"Miss Bailey is an important part of my campaign team, Mr. Roberts," he said, looking at her with praise in his eyes and hoping to put an end to it, but the other man didn't take the hint.

"Oh yes! I can imagine just what sort of important role Miss Bailey must play on your team. That would be your personal team, right, Mike?"

Michael could feel an angry heat rise into his face. He felt bad for Kendall to be sitting there while a man completely dismissed her valuable contributions to his campaign. He could see her stiffen, and if getting these men's money wasn't so important to the campaign, he would have told them just where they could go. His displeasure must have been obvious because Mr. Ramos stepped in to defuse the situation by asking everyone to take their seats.

Michael couldn't decide which of the men he would rather risk Kendall sitting next to. She selected for herself and sat on the end of the table next to Michael and opposite the young, quiet retailer.

"You looked like you were going to kill Mr. Roberts," she whispered into his ear when no one was listening.

"The night is still young," Michael whispered back. "I'm pretty sure I can remember all of my army training."

The protectiveness in his comment made Kendall smile. Dinner went painfully slow. Nobody seemed to be in any hurry to start talking business, but Kendall had a feeling Michael was just being polite. It wasn't a subject that was even raised until they were waiting for dessert to arrive, and then after a perfectly pleasant, albeit a dull couple of hours, no one could agree on anything.

This part of campaigning was all new to Kendall. She was normally a much more behind-the-scenes kind of gal, but she had an idea in her head how it all worked. What she hadn't expected was the ridiculously small amount of money they were willing to donate to the party, especially when she heard what they expected Michael to give them in return. She was surprised, but also impressed, by how calm and composed Michael was while listening to their offers. Perhaps he had been expecting this? As crazy as the idea seemed, Kendall tried to avoid politics outside of work. She approached her job as a marketing problem. That was how she managed to jump from one campaign to another in an upwardly mobile arc. She tried to give both sides of an issue equal weight, so she could take whatever position that was assigned. Listening to Michael, however, it was impossible not to pay attention to the problems he raised, or to feel intrigued by the solutions that he proposed.

After dinner, drinks came and went as the evening became increasingly late. It was apparent that nothing was going to be decided on tonight and Kendall hoped this meant she and Michael could leave soon. She still had a few hours of work to do on the speech, which she was determined to finish by the next morning on principle.

Before Kendall could get Michael's attention and give him the "are we done yet?" look that couples exchange so discreetly, the maitre d' hurried into the room and spoke quietly into Mr. Ramos's ear. The hotelier frowned, and then laughed before he turned to speak to Michael.

"Well, Mike, It seems you won't be escaping back to Louisville until we have reached an agreement after all."

"Oh?" Michael questioned. He sounded curious and mildly amused, but Kendall had seen his shoulders tense.

"Look!" Ramos laughed, getting up from the dinner table and then walking across the room to the large windows. He pulled back the heavy drapes, which had been drawn to afford them more privacy, and revealed the beginnings of a raging thunderstorm outside.

"Oh my God!" Kendall exclaimed as a flash of lightning split the sky.

"It's okay," Ramos chuckled. "It is just a spin-off from a tropical storm further down the coast. It wasn't supposed to turn northward, but we got unlucky. My assistant just told me that he spoke with your pilot. All outbound flights have been grounded due to wind shear."

Kendall and her date exchanged glances. Michael had a wicked little grin that he was trying to suppress, but it was not lost on her. Were they really stranded here together? A shiver traveled down Kendall's spine, and it didn't have anything to do with the electrical storm.

"Then it appears we will have to trespass on your hospitality for a little longer, Ernesto," Michael said, frowning out at the storm.

"It's not a problem. I'm sure that I can rustle up someplace for you to stay," he assured them. "Give me a minute to work something out," he said, and then left the restaurant. Kendall assumed that he had gone to sort out their room... *rooms?*

"Michael?" Kendall whispered. Only she and Michael had followed Ramos to look out of the window. The other men were too busy drinking and joking to pay them any attention. "Michael we can't share a room!" she hissed, trying and failing to deny the attractions of the idea.

Michael looked down at her with one eyebrow raised.

"Why not? You are my girlfriend, after all," he said in a low voice.

"But- but don't you think it might do more harm than good? If it comes out that we stayed here... *together?* You know someone from the hotel will talk to the press and tell them there was only one room," Kendall croaked. She really wasn't as concerned over what people would think, it had more to do with being alone in a room with Michael and having some self-control.

Michael slid his hands into his pockets, looked out at the storm and rocked back on his heels. There was a smile dancing over his lips that Kendall wasn't sure she trusted. "No, I don't think so, not if you're going to marry me," he said matter-of-factly.

"Not if I'm *what?*" Kendall's eyes almost popped out of her head. Michael shot her a warning glance, and Kendall lowered her voice, remembering that they weren't alone in the room. "What do you mean?" she hissed quietly. *"Not if I'm going to marry you?"*

"Not really of course," Michael whispered, managing to speak almost without moving his lips. "But that's what we can say if we're caught. It might be worth running with that angle regardless," he mused, looking thoughtful. "You know, in for a penny, in for a pound. Doesn't the saying go something like that?"

Kendall wasn't sure if she should be insulted or flattered. "Now you want us to pretend to get engaged?" she whispered incredulously.

"You would get a very nice ring out of the bargain," Michael chuckled. "You could even keep it when all of this is over."

"How generous," Kendall snorted. "How exactly is all of this going to end, Michael?" she demanded, forgetting again that they weren't alone. "Because we're going to find ourselves walking down the aisle at this rate!"

"Don't be ridiculous. It will never get that far." Michael smiled and alerted Kendall to Mr. Ramos's return so that she wouldn't continue with the topic.

"The room is ready for you," Ramos announced, walking over to the couple. "Would you like for my staff to show you up now, or wait until later?"

*M*ichael and Kendall were coaxed into staying for drinks. They tried to wrap up the after-dinner conversation but still didn't manage to get away for another hour, and when they did finally excuse themselves, Mr. Ramos insisted on showing them up to their room himself.

Michael was disappointed to see their 'room' was, in fact, two separate bedrooms, connected by a sitting room and a large, luxurious shared bathroom.

"Wow," Kendall whispered as Ramos quickly showed them around. She was no stranger to nice hotel rooms when she traveled, but this went beyond the standard suite upgrade. "This place is bigger than my first apartment!"

Michael grinned.

"If you need anything, anything at all, just call room service. Your wish is their command," Ramos said. "Don't worry about the bill. We'll call it part of my donation," he chuckled before bidding them goodnight.

"I don't like him," Kendall said, as soon as their host

was gone. "He's sure to tell someone! And if he doesn't, surely someone on his staff will. Some gossip writer is probably working on a story right now to post online by midnight," she rambled anxiously.

Michael stared at her incredulously. "Kendall, I think you're overreacting a bit. There are two beds in this suite. We're not exactly staying here by choice. If you wanted to, you could go and lock yourself in your half of the suite."

It was Kendall's turned to stare up at Michael incredulously. "As if that would be possible," she slipped, and then her cheeks began to burn a fiery red. "Please forget I said that," she said, fanning him away as she put some distance between them.

"Oh, I don't think so," Michael grinned. "I want to know exactly what that meant," he teased.

"Just that- only that- everyone thinks we're a couple," she managed to get out. "And what couple- I mean, what genuine couple would stay in a hotel like this- in a room like this and sleep in separate beds?"

"An interesting question," Michael agreed, his voice had dropped to a low rumbling purr. "Is there an answer?"

"Well- I mean, it doesn't apply to us!" Kendall gasped, a little desperately.

"But it does. At least the rest of the world thinks so. You agreed to go along with this, why do you care what everyone else thinks? Especially when everyone thinks we're only doing what a couple naturally does."

Michael made a good point, but Kendall was feeling flustered all the same. She hadn't prepared for the evening to turn out like this. It was becoming a bit overwhelming. The flight, the fancy dinner, the fancy suite...

She was supposed to be on a flight back to Kentucky right now, but instead she found herself getting caught up in the excitement of it all.

"We are supposed to be setting a higher standard for our country. Most importantly though, we're not really a- not really a-" but she couldn't finish, because Michael had just pulled her into his arms and crushed her lips beneath his mouth.

Kendall gasped in surprise, and given an opening, Michael's tongue surged powerfully between her teeth. She hadn't been prepared for the kiss- so she was even more unprepared for the hungry, practically ravenous way that Michael stole her mouth, but she wasn't about to complain. After a moment of resistance, she wrapped her arms tightly around his neck.

"There aren't any cameras here," Michael murmured against her neck.

Kendall thought there was a question in his voice, but she was too confused to make out his meaning. "What?"

His breath puffed against the nape of her neck, the heat of it seeming to melt into Kendall's body and pool inside her gut.

"I mean there's no reason to act...Do you want me to stop?"

Kendall answered with a groan. She didn't have a clue what Michael was up to, but she was already craving more.

"We could probably use some practice..." she answered in a husky whisper.

The sound of her voice had barely faded before Michael buried her in another heavy kiss. His arm circled around her waist, crushing her against his chest, and all of his famous cool and control was gone in an instant.

Michael took what he wanted from her without being terribly concerned about giving anything in return. At least at first. His mouth was harsh, almost cruel, bruising in the force with which it moved against the plump bow of Kendall's lips. Instead of wanting to pull away from him, however, Kendall gave herself up completely to Michael's control. She let him kiss her until she was literally breathless and weak, pretending that she had a choice in the matter. Then, his hands began to move.

"Michael?" Kendall barely recognized her breathless, throaty voice.

"Don't talk," he commanded, his voice had deepened to a low, velvety purr that hummed through Kendall's body. "Just-" but he didn't finish speaking. He covered her mouth again, and let his hands and lips tell her what he wanted.

Kendall allowed a small moan to escape her lips as Michael's palms swept heavily over her curves. There was nothing gentle about his touch, it was sure and greedy, just like his kisses, and Kendall was both shocked and aroused by the certainty with which he was assaulting her body. She wasn't sure that she had the will power to keep herself in check and stop him from taking what he wanted. Nor did she really want to.

"You feel amazing," Michael rasped, moving from her lips to place a line of heavy kisses all the way along her jaw and down her throat. That was where his mouth moved at least, his hands were busily involved in groping Kendall's breasts. They kneaded the sensitive flesh roughly, making Kendall gasp and moan in wanton pleasure.

She knew that she shouldn't let him treat her like this- like an object at his sexual disposal- but she couldn't help it. She wanted to give in to her baser desires. Was this really happening? She couldn't quite reconcile where they were in the moment versus where they were heading, and she was split between the mind of wanting to know and wanting to stop before they both did something that would complicate matters even more. She was being steered toward the bed, and they tumbled down together, limbs entwined.

"I want to see you naked," he growled, slipping his hands under the hem of her dress and pushing it up her thighs. Every nerve in her body was on fire, and she was acutely aware of even the smallest detail, like the feeling of the silky material skating up against her skin as he pushed it higher and higher.

"Fucking hell," Michael swore, as he revealed the tiny scrap of black silk edged with red ribbon, which passed for Kendall's panties. "Who were you wearing these for?" he questioned possessively as he ran a finger over the damp material, causing Kendall to arch up off the bed.

"Who?" Michael whispered this time, taking pleasure in the fact Kendall could only whimper incoherently.

"No one-" she gasped, moaning more loudly when Michael pushed the fabric aside and began to rub her sex.

"I think you did it for me," he breathed into her ear, pressing his body down on top of hers so that she could feel the jutting hardness of his cock. "I think you want me as much as I want you."

Kendall shivered again, but she couldn't quite bring herself to answer Michael and admit the truth. In some small part of her mind she continued to lie to herself and believe that in the end, she wouldn't give in to Michael. She would not give in to the aching desire that had been building for days. She couldn't answer him with words, and her body betrayed her anyway, her hips rocking up against him. Desperate little whimpers came tumbling from her lips, and she smiled every time she heard his voice urging her on. Wetness had pooled between her legs as Michael's fingers continued to roughly fondle her sex.

"That's so fucking hot, how wet you are right now," he growled approvingly. "How long have you been aching for me?"

"Michael!" she managed to groan.

Michael's free hand pushed Kendall's dress higher up her body, revealing her flat belly just before uncovering her silk-clad breasts. The groan he made on seeing her, coupled with the lust that was so blatant on his face, made her muscles clench involuntarily.

"Sit up," he ordered, withdrawing his hands from her body, but only temporarily.

Kendall gave a frustrated moan, but she obeyed. The moment she did her dress was whipped over her head and tossed onto the floor. The raw male appreciation on Michael's face couldn't possibly be feigned. How his eyes roamed over her exposed flesh didn't embarrass her, as she thought it might, but only made her desire for him grow. Soon he seemed fixated on the heavy, swollen mounds of her breasts.

"I need to-" he started to say but didn't finish explaining what he needed before he simply took it. His hands were suddenly on Kendall's breasts, cupping the luscious swells through the silk of her bra. They were the sure, certain hands of a man who knew exactly want he wanted- of a man who had no intention of stopping until he had what he wanted.

Michael lowered his head, and Kendall gasped with pleasure as the hot wet center of his mouth latched onto her nipple and began suckling her through the fabric of her bra. His hands slipped under her back, seeking out the clasp, while his mouth worked at melting Kendall to the core.

"God, you're gorgeous," Michael hissed, for a second when his mouth was free. "I always knew you were beautiful, but I didn't know you'd do this to me," he grunted, grinding the huge bulge in his pants against her belly.

He felt tremendous.

"You did that," Michael rasped. He stripped away Kendall's bra, leaving her lying behind him in just her panties and stockings. She felt on display yet powerful in her femininity, pinned beneath the weight of his still clothed body.

"I want to see you too," she finally found her voice just as Michael buried his head between her breasts again. The shock of feeling his tongue on her naked skin made her body jerk and shudder. "Please..." she begged, twisting her fingers in his hair and tugging his head.

Michael pulled back enough to look at her flushed face. "What do you want to see?" he teased, a smug smile tugging on his lips. He captured Kendall's hand and drew it to his crotch, pressed her fingers against the tented material and urging her to explore the stiff, pulsing shaft that lay beneath.

"Oh God," she panted, squirming around as she traced his length and width. She couldn't stay still; her body was quite literally throbbing to be possessed by his monstrous sex. "I want to see-" she gasped greedily, reaching with shaky fingers for his belt.

For a second, Kendall thought that Michael was going to stop her, but after a pause, he simply nodded and began to unbutton his own shirt while she struggled with his belt. Her fingers were so clumsy with desire and excitement that Michael had his shirt off before she had even mastered the buckle. It was a delicious treat when she finally looked up to discover the muscled expanse of skin in front of her.

"Oh my..." she purred appreciatively, lifting one hand and raking it through the crisp, black whirl of hair that covered his chest.

The heat of Michael's skin, the masculine scent of him, and the beat of his heart behind her palm were almost too much for Kendall to bear. She took a moment to appreciate the hard lines and definition you usually only see on movie stars. It was the kind of body that you look at and only dream of touching. If she were this turned on by only seeing half of it, she wasn't sure how much self-control she'd be able to muster once she was able to take in the entire package.

Michael obviously didn't have the patience to sit and wait for her to finish admiring him, however. He grabbed her hand again and reminded her what she had been in the middle of doing. "I want to feel your hands on my cock." What should have been a crude statement only excited her even more.

"Only my hands?" Kendall whispered provocatively.

Michael smiled wickedly, helping Kendall with his belt. "Well, we have to start somewhere." As soon as it was unbuckled Kendall's eager fingers darted for his fly. The zipper eased down without issue, and when she popped open the waistband of his pants, her breath caught in surprise.

Michael wasn't wearing any underwear.

If Kendall had lifted her gaze and looked at his face, she would have noted the very smug, satisfied smiled fixed there, but as it was, she was far too transfixed by the sight of his cock to drag her eyes away.

"This isn't a spectator sport, sweetheart," Michael urged, alerting Kendall to the fact that she hadn't moved for several seconds.

She licked her lips and reached for him, maintaining eye contact as she did. She was instantly gratified by the way that Michael's whole body shuddered at the first fluttering touch of her fingertips. It was empowering to watch the look of satisfaction on his face, to feel like she was taking a bit of control over the situation.

"So big," she purred approvingly, making enthusiastic little murmurs and whimpers as she stroked him with one hand. Her other hand dropped down between his legs to lightly caress his balls.

Michael struggled not to thrust his hips into Kendall's soft, silky palm as he reveled in the feeling of her touch. His own hands reached for her, cupping her breasts and fondling her ass, as she continued to explore him. The dampness between her thighs had her squirming uncomfortably, and her agitation seemed to capture Michael's attention.

Kendall squealed as Michael pushed her down onto the mattress, tipping her over onto her back without warning. "I want to be here," he rasped, pressing his knuckles against her sodden panties.

"I want you there too," Kendall urged him on and sighed with relief when he stripped her naked. He stroked her a few times and then thrust a finger into her sheath. It wasn't enough. The heat had built so much that the only thing to satisfy her now was to feel his large, hard cock inside her.

"I don't want to hurt you," Michael admitted, pinning

her hands to her sides when she tried to reach for his cock and guide him inside.

"Please, Michael," she moaned, thinking that he might very well split her in half, but she was past the point of caring.

Kendall rolled her hips towards him and spread her legs a touch wider. That was it. Michael was undone. Growling something she couldn't decipher, he settled into the cradle she had created for him. He tangled one hand in her hair, angling her mouth for a deep kiss as he dragged his shaft through the wet heat that glistened between Kendall's legs. He repeated the movement, once, twice more, before finding her opening and pushing inside. He thrust shallowly at first, sucking on Kendall's bottom lip, as he eased just the head of his sex into her hungry body.

"You want more?" he whispered, his voice rough and unsteady.

"Yes, please!" Kendall cried, mindless with the need that he had created inside of her.

Michael hesitated just for a second, then pressed his lips firmly to her temple as he thrust forwards as deeply as he could manage- impaling her. Kendall gasped from the shock of being possessed so completely. Her muscles struggled to accommodate him as Michael touched places that no other man had ever reached before. It wasn't the pain of his entrance that made Kendall lose her breath, although there was a sharp sting of soreness as he forced her to take virtually the whole length of his sex, it was the sheer intensity of being so wonderfully filled. It felt incredible. Whole.

Michael didn't immediately rear back. He stilled inside Kendall's sheath, giving her a moment to get used to his length and girth. What that cost him, she would never know, although the strain on him was visible to see in his face. His eyes were clenched shut, and the tendons in his neck were straining. Kendall gave her hips an experimental wriggle, gasping again when she realized how impossibly sensitive her body felt.

"Are you trying to fucking kill me?" Michael growled when she increased the movements of her hips.

"I'm just having a little fun," she teased, taking advantage of his moment of restraint but then he turned the tables and finally started to move. Kendall had thought that she was ready for him, but the first few plunges of his cock still brought with them that fine line between pleasure and pain as her body became used to him being inside her.

"Oh, God!" She was shocked to realize how close she already was to breaking. Her hips matched Michael thrust for thrust, and she was unaware of her fingernails digging into the sweaty skin of his back as she tried to bring him closer... closer to orgasm, closer to her body, she wasn't quite sure.

"Fucking hell," Michael cursed, groaning as the already tight walls of Kendall's sheath continued to tighten, nearing her release.

"Michael! Please!" she begged. "Michael... I can't... I'm going to..." and then she was coming, erupting in spasms of pleasure.

He didn't stop, he couldn't. He didn't even slow his tempo. If anything, the speed, and force with which he was taking her increased so that he was powering Kendall's orgasm to keep going, propelling her to an even more intense sphere of feeling.

"Oh my God, Michael!" she sobbed, her back arching

against the mattress as he forced her body to endure the continuing bursts of pleasure. She knew why the French called it la petit mort now! She couldn't possibly stay conscious and withstand such pleasure.

Kendall's body shattered again. Her hips kept rising, still throbbing with satisfaction, but the rest of her was limp with ecstasy. Michael hadn't quite finished yet though, he kept grinding forward, rutting like an animal as he chased his own release. Finally, he jerked to a stop and let out a low, deep, guttural groan that sounded as if it was torn from somewhere deep inside him. It renewed her with enough strength to wrap her shaking legs around him, binding them together as his body shuddered completely. The hot eruption was just enough to prove to be Kendall's undoing. She had never felt so close to passing out from pleasure in her life.

"Fuck, fuck, *oh fuck*," panted Michael, just before his legs and arms gave out. He was almost crushing her with his large body, but she was too dazed to care. If she died right here and now, she would die a very happy woman.

"I think you've ruined me," she sighed, slurring her words as if she was drunk.

Michael's eyes snapped open, bright with guilt and concern, both of which Kendall failed to notice.

"What?" His voice was rough but a bit shaky.

"I had no idea sex was meant to feel like that," she purred.

Michael couldn't help but smile at that remark. It had been utterly sensational, he had to admit. He kissed Kendall's cheek, and eased a little of his weight off her, although he was reluctant to pull away completely. He liked the feel of her body tucked under him.

"Obviously you haven't been having it with the right man," he said, dabbing a kiss against her swollen lips.

Kendall smiled up at him softly, her skin was still beautifully flushed, and her hair was in disarray. "No, obviously not," she sighed, looking absolutely drugged with pleasure.

"I'm sorry if I hurt you," he apologized quietly, rolling onto his side and taking Kendall with him. He had tried to be gentle in the beginning, but her body responded to him in such a way that urged him on. She looked so beautiful beneath him, skin flushed and sweat beading down her body while he moved inside her, the temptation not to completely take her had been too immense, and he wasn't sure he hadn't been a little too rough.

"Don't be sorry," Kendall laughed, putting his slight fears at ease. She gave a wicked, naughty little giggle that made the hair on the back of Michael's neck stand on end and then curled up to lay her head on his chest. "It was perfect," she whispered, drawing nonsensical patterns on his skin with her fingertips.

"Mmmm," Michael agreed sleepily. He shut his eyes and yawned deeply then wrapped his arms around Kendall's waist and settled down to sleep for what was left of the night. The last thing he remembered was looking across the room out the window. The storm was over, and moonlight was peeking between the cloud.

11

Michael groaned, the sunlight poured through a crack in the curtains and hit him square in the face. It was far too early to be awake, and he felt like he hadn't slept for more than a couple of hours. Even though his mind was hazy, he was aware of the soft white sheets that were different from the ones at home. He was used to sleeping in different beds on the campaign trail, normally they weren't quite this nice. He was just about to take a deep breath and settle back into the warmth of the bed when he remembered the reason why he felt like he hadn't slept for more than a handful of minutes.

Michael was instantly wide-awake. And more than one part of him had realized that it was high time to be getting up. He considered surprising her with an encore of last night, especially since she continued to push her warm backside up against his body. There's no way she was asleep, she had to be doing it on purpose.

"Kendall?" He whispered, his breath warm against her ear. There was no movement, so he whispered again, this time running his hand down the length of her naked side and coming to rest on the curve of her hip. This time she stirred.

One eye fluttered open, and Michael watched the smile develop on her face as the realization of where she was and who she was with came over her. It was sweet.

It was also short-lived.

Kendall flipped over quickly, and the entire mood disappeared as quick as it came. "What did we do? How could I let this happen? What if someone finds out," she started immediately, easing herself out of bed and taking the bedsheet with her as she went. Michael thought it was amusing that she was suddenly so shy.

"Good morning to you too," Michael said with a yawn. "Don't worry, no one is going to find out." He sat up and swung his legs over the side of the bed, unselfconscious of his nakedness as he rubbed the sleep from his eyes. There was nothing shy about Michael. "It might help my reputation if people did though!"

"It would ruin your reputation! Do we have to go over this again?" Kendall called from the bathroom.

"Because two consenting adults decided to have a little fun?" he called back towards the bathroom. She didn't respond, but he knew she was right. He just couldn't find it in himself to care right now. He was feeling far, far too good. Obviously, a night of mind-blowing sex was just what he had needed to recharge his batteries. Now, he could focus again.

"We have a little problem," Kendall said, walking back out of the ensuite bathroom. She exchanged the sheet for one of the hotel's fluffy white robes. Michael preferred the sheet.

"Another one?" he grinned.

Kendall didn't return the smile. "We don't have any clean clothes."

"Oh dear," Michael said, struggling to keep a straight face. "I suppose we'll just have to stay naked then."

"Michael!" Kendall cried, eyes flashing dangerously at him.

He held up his hands in surrender. "It's fine. It won't be a problem. I'll get it sorted," he promised so that to appease her.

Kendall looked doubtful but decided not to question him. She wasn't sure she wanted to know how he was going to get it sorted. Instead, she returned to the bathroom and climbed into the bath that she had been running for herself.

The warm water felt heavenly against her skin. It soothed the tender flesh between her legs and enveloped her entire body as she lay back and let the water level rise above her skin. She closed her eyes and let her mind wander, it immediately went to Michael. Where do things go from here? Having sex with Michael wasn't expected as part of their deal. She knew that. They were way over the line, and Tom would blow a gasket if he ever found out, but was their "mistake" just the result of playing pretend and getting caught up in the performance? Michael had described it in very unflattering terms earlier. *Two consenting adults having a little fun.* Was that all they were doing? Having fun? Could she be okay with that?

Kendall lathered up a bar of soap between her hands and tried to think about the situation rationally. She wasn't going to be silly and emotional about it. It was only sex after all... and really, *really* good sex at that. She had to weigh her options carefully and not make any rash decisions.

After Kendall washed her body and her hair, she climbed out of the bathtub, wrapped a large fluffy towel around herself and padded back into the bedroom. Michael hadn't left the bed but had his cell phone pressed to his ear. From the sound of things he seemed to be speaking to Thomas.

Kendall would have been content to just stand there and watch him, drinking in the sight of his naked chest and tousled hair, but Michael waved a hand when he spotted her and directed her to a few large boxes that were sitting just inside the door. Looking puzzled, Kendall wandered over, picked them up and carried them over to the bed before lifting the lids.

"Oooh!" she cooed when she saw what was inside. It was an exquisite red silk dress, and in the other boxes she uncovered matching shoes, a coat, and matching bra and panty set. She tried not to squeal like a little girl with each new discovery and hadn't even been paying attention to the man on the bed with her until Michael leaned across and prodded her with his foot. She glanced up at him in confusion.

"No, Tom... Well, it must be the TV... No! Of course not. Why would Miss Bailey be in the room with me?" he asked innocently.

Kendall flushed guiltily and took her goodies away with her into the other bedroom to change. She didn't have a clue how Michael had known what sizes to ask for, but he had somehow managed perfectly. She chose to believe that he must have glanced in the labels of the clothes that were strewn about the room, but she had a nasty suspicion that he might just be so familiar with women and their bodies that he would simply be able to tell.

Once she was dressed again, Kendall managed to fix her hair, but she didn't have any makeup apart from a lipstick that she always carried in her purse. Fortunately, the night's activities lent a rosy glow to her cheeks and so she didn't feel too self-conscious when she wandered back into the other room bare-faced to see what Michael was doing.

The bed was empty, and she heard water spraying in the bathroom. For a split second, Kendall wished she hadn't bathed already so she could surprise Michael in the shower. Then she wondered if that would be inappropriate. Last night it didn't seem like anything would be out of bounds, but in the light of morning, she wasn't sure. Were they supposed to act like nothing happened and get back on track with the Operation Girlfriend plan?

Kendall forced herself to stop overthinking everything and noticed that there was a clean suit tossed over the back of a chair. She took a closer peek, giggling to herself when she noted a definite lack of boxer shorts.

A wicked thought popped into her head. What if in all the time that she had known Michael, at all the staff meetings, all the rallies, and all the interviews he had always been gloriously naked under his pants? The thought made her hot and light-headed.

As if Kendall hadn't been feeling giddy enough, Michael himself emerged from the bathroom a second later wearing nothing but a towel haphazardly knotted about his waist. The sight of him, clean and freshly shaven, made Kendall want to dirty him up again. He smiled when he saw her and then started to rub his hair dry with a hand towel.

"I should go and turn the bed down in the other room," Kendall said, hoping that this might at least buy them the appearance of having slept in different beds.

Michael raised a doubtful eyebrow. He glanced at the bed that they had slept in. The messy, tainted sheets didn't leave anything to the imagination. He sniffed the air too, alerting Kendall to the fact that the room still smelled like sex. She shrugged her shoulders and flung open a couple of windows.

"Hey!" Michael yelped, as he was nearly blinded by the sudden burst of bright sunlight in his eyes.

"I'm only thinking of your reputation, Mr. Reese," Kendall said innocently, earning a growl from the man, as he watched her disappear.

She went straight to the other bedroom and tried to make the bed look as though it had been slept in. She threw the blankets about a bit and dented one of the pillows, but she couldn't help thinking that it still looked suspicious. For a moment, she considered climbing on top of it and jumping around like a child.

"Oh well," she sighed, hoping that she was simply over-anxious. No maid was going to pay too much attention to the state of the beds, right?

Trying not to dwell on the precarious nature of their position, Kendall decided to keep herself busy while she waited for Michael to finish dressing. She didn't imagine that it would take him long, but she took her iPad out of her purse to see what she could do about the speech.

In the end, Kendall had plenty of time to work on Michael's speech. She heard his cell phone ring several times, and he hadn't stopped talking in the other room since she left him. Kendall wondered if he had even managed to dress. Once she talked herself out of checking, she engrossed herself in writing. There wasn't much work left to do, and she managed to finish the whole thing just before she heard Michael calling her name.

"What were you doing in there?" he asked, straightening his tie and pulling on his jacket.

Kendall held up her iPad triumphantly. "I'm sorry this isn't 'on your desk,' but I'm afraid you can't have everything."

Michael raised an eyebrow. "The speech?" he asked, sounding impressed. "I told you not to worry about that."

"Well, I know, but you were right. It's my job."

Michael smiled with approval and Kendall felt about ten feet tall.

"I'll have a glance at it over breakfast?"

"Breakfast?" Kendall scrunched up her nose and glanced at her watch.

"Fine, brunch?" Michael conceded, ushering her towards the door. "I need to eat something to keep up my strength if I'm going to be spending the rest of the day with you."

12

_M_ichael and Kendall ate brunch together in the hotel restaurant, conscious of the need not to draw unwanted attention to themselves. To anyone watching, it looked like nothing more than a normal business luncheon. Michael read through the speech that Kendall had prepared while he drank copious amounts of coffee. He made a few minor alterations to phrasing. Overall, he was immensely pleased with her work.

He was pleased with _everything_ about Kendall, Michael reflected on the flight back to Kentucky. He couldn't have made a better choice of 'pretend' girlfriend.

It turned out that the public agreed with him.

Over the following days, Kendall charmed men and connected with women all over the country. Tom declared that she was the key to 'softening' Michael's image. Before Kendall, the Candidate had been seen as a tough war veteran or a ruthless lady's man, but now, his female companion was able to bring something fresh and new to the plate. Through her, Michael could lay claim to a more caring, compassionate side. As much as Michael hated to admit it, Tom's plan was working flawlessly.

"They are lapping it up!" Tom beamed, bursting into Michael's office late one Friday afternoon.

"Who are lapping what up?" Michael asked distractedly, not turning his head away from the laptop he was giving so much attention too. He was leaving on a week-long campaign trip the following day and was just looking over the schedule. Every second was crammed full. Normally he liked it that way. The busier he was, the less trouble he could get into, but he didn't see any time to meet up with Kendall. It was aggravating.

In fact, he hadn't managed to snatch more than a couple of minutes alone with Kendall since they returned from Washington. Michael frequently fell asleep reliving the time they had shared in the nation's Capital. He wanted to repeat the experience and prove to himself that he hadn't imagined the sparks that had flown that night, but there had never been another opportunity. He was hoping that would change soon, but it was looking less and less likely.

"...don't you think, Michael? *Michael*!" The boom of Tom's voice finally regained his attention.

"I'm sorry, what were you saying?" Michael asked apologetically. "Something about licking?"

"*Lapping*! And that was five minutes ago!" Tom snapped. "I was talking about Kendall."

Michael's attention was suddenly riveted. "What about Kendall?" he asked, trying to keep his voice casual. He got the feeling that Tom suspected something had happened between Michael and Kendall in D.C., particularly because it was almost always Tom who found a reason to separate them when they did manage to grab a moment alone.

"I was telling you what a positive impact she's had on your approval rating," Tom sighed wearily. "Just as I predicted she would."

"Great," Michael grinned. "I never doubted you for a second, Tom." They both knew that wasn't true, but Michael wanted to give Tom the credit for it now that things were running more smoothly.

"Anyway, I think it's time I drew up a list of different things for her to do- visits, speeches, that kind of thing."

Michael nodded slowly. He wasn't sure how Kendall would feel about that. He already got the impression she wasn't thrilled about all the time away from her 'real job.'

"When were you thinking of having her start?" Michael asked. "After we finish the campaign trip?"

"She's not going on the campaign trip, Michael."

Michael's expression darkened. "What do you mean, 'she's not going on the campaign trip'?" he growled. "You just told me she was helping my approval rating."

Tom raised his eyebrows at Michael's reaction and shook his head. "This is precisely why Miss Bailey isn't coming, Michael," he said sternly. "She's a distraction you can't afford."

I'm not distracted! I'm frustrated! Michael felt like yelling at the man but instead tried a different approach. "Thomas, look-," he started to speak while trying to regain his calm, but he was interrupted.

"Not to mention the fact that the Vance campaign will tear you apart if you go cavorting around with a woman who is not your wife!"

"There are plenty of women on the team who travel with us, Tom," Michael pointed out. "Hell! Kendall used to travel around with us before you installed her as my girlfriend! Besides, we don't 'cavort'!" *That you know about,* he added silently.

"You aren't having a 'relationship' with any of the other women on the team," Norm pointed out calmly.

Michael knew that what Thomas said was true. He couldn't flaunt his relationship with Kendall. He couldn't risk giving the impression that their relationship was sexual, especially if they were just dating. The current sitting President had nearly been toppled by a scandal during the second year of his term and Tom had been adamant that Michael would not have an incident like that taint his campaign. Michael sighed heavily and admitted defeat.

"Okay, Tom, you win," Michael grunted. "You want me to go and tell Kendall what her new duties are?" he asked, eyeing the paper that Tom was holding.

"Well no, I think I can probably manage-" the older man muttered, backing out of the office before Michael could impose his will.

Michael couldn't help being irritated. If Tom were twenty years younger, then he would seriously consider him a rival for Kendall's affections. *Not that Michael was interested in her affections so to speak.* He just resented any other man hovering around her like Tom tended to do.

Now Michael was in a foul mood as he turned his attention back to the schedule. When the telephone rang half an hour later his voice was cross when he said 'hello'.

"Is this a bad time?" Kendall asked.

Michael cursed under his breath. "No, of course not, Kendall. What can I do for you?"

"I've just been speaking to Thomas-"

Michael glanced at his watch and frowned again. Kendall had been talking to Tom all this time?

"- and I wanted to know what you think of me taking on a more active role in your campaign?"

Michael could hear the uncertainty in her voice and wished that he could see her face.

"I think you'll do an excellent job," he said honestly. "I can't imagine trusting anyone else to do it."

"Well, except perhaps your real girlfriend," Kendall pointed out dryly.

"If I had one you mean?" Michael chuckled.

"Well yes, there *is* that," Kendall agreed, a little hurt at the reminder of their sham even though she brought it up. She shook it off and went for a lighter route. "Perhaps one day you'll meet the woman of your dreams and live happily ever after," she said in a mocking, sing-song tone.

He could hear a small smile in her voice which made him relax a bit. He hadn't even realized his back had been so tense until he settled comfortably into his chair to continue their conversation.

Kendall brought the conversation back to work. "Tom also mentioned that this means I'm off the campaign trip," she added quietly.

"Yeah, well-" Michael cleared his throat. "You can understand why it's necessary?" he asked, not willing to admit that Tom had dropped that bombshell on him too. Frankly, Tom's 'orders' were starting to piss Michael off. "But I'll call you? And I'll email."

"You will?" Kendall asked, sounding doubtful.

"Sure I will. It will be fun."

PLAYING pen pals with Michael *was* fun, although

Kendall hardly dared admit that to herself. Regardless of how she tried to explain the way her heart skipped a beat whenever her phone chimed with a new e-mail, it was becoming impossible to deny that she was checking her inbox with increasing frequency as the days of Michael's trip went by. When the first email arrived, she was surprised by the giddy feeling it gave her. *Yes*, Michael had said that he would write to her, but somehow, she hadn't really believed him. She found it hard to picture Michael sitting down at a computer tapping away to tell her about his day. She always thought that he ought to be doing something more active.

However, despite this mental picture that Kendall had concocted, Michael proved to be a very faithful correspondent. His emails started off politely and properly enough. He talked about his travels: what he had done, what he had achieved, and what was scheduled next. He asked about her day and not just work-related issues. He seemed to be genuinely curious about what she'd been up to in her free time. It didn't take Michael more than a day or two to change the tune of his emails and wander down a different route entirely.

Instead of asking her what she was doing, he asked her what she was wearing- followed by a detailed description of what he *wasn't* wearing.

Kendall knew that she should delete Michael's emails and never answer them, but not because she didn't want them. She couldn't risk having them discovered by a third party. They would be dangerous in the wrong hands. Stuff like that happened too often in political campaigns. The IT department had warned them all endlessly about the perils of attempted hacking. The warnings echoed in her mind every time she opened a new note. Despite knowing better, she couldn't bring herself to delete Michael's letters. They were her guilty pleasure. She reread them, over and over again, growing hot and bothered from Michael's words no matter how many times she reviewed the same message. She found herself yearning for the time when she and Michael would be able to act out some of the scintillating scenarios that he had created and planted in her mind.

Every day Kendall made the same promise to herself, that she wouldn't immediately rush to check her email as soon as she woke up or continue to check her phone compulsively during work hours. Every day Kendall failed miserably. It was to the point that she couldn't even escape while she slept. Michael always found a way to creep inside her dreams and warm her body at night.

Kendall tried to ignore the way that her heart picked up speed when she looked at the small rectangular screen of her phone and saw an email alert. A quick tap, and there it was: an e-mail from Michael Reese. The name was spelled out in bold letters under the "new messages" column. She felt like a whole swarm of butterflies were fluttering around inside her stomach when she clicked open the email and started to read.

13

"*R*oom service!"
Michael grabbed his robe off the bed. Housekeeping startled him in the middle of a particularly well-crafted erotic message to Kendall. The evidence of his arousal was still apparent through his robe, so he snapped his computer shut and held it on his lap before calling for the maid to enter.

"Good morning, Mr. Reese," the cheerful young housekeeper called out as she stepped through the door. She laid out his breakfast and a selection of newspapers on a nearby table and asked if there was anything else he needed before she went on her way.

What he needed was Kendall. Michael groaned, wondering how he had gotten himself into this mess. He was in the race of his life, trying to win an election that would impact the lives of millions of people. This was no time for distractions, but he couldn't get his would-be First Lady out of his head. He glanced at his watch and saw that it was almost time for Kendall's appearance on a morning talk show. He *ought* to spend his precious free time reviewing notes for the rally that evening, or studying the morning polls, but once the image of Kendall was fixed in his mind, resistance was futile. He flicked on the TV, deciding to savor a few stolen minutes of hedonistic pleasure before getting to work.

Michael took a sip of coffee and turned his eyes to the television. He was only vaguely aware of the program, letting his mind travel back to the night he and Kendall had spent together. He was just about to let himself get carried away with the mental image of her bare body beneath him when he heard Kendall's voice and snapped back to reality as she came into focus on the screen.

She was wearing a pale blue skirt suit, and her hair was pulled into a stylish chignon. She looked perfectly gorgeous. Perhaps too perfect. Was that possible? He wanted to pull the pins from her hair and smudge her make up. He wanted her like she had been in D.C. - a sexual, sensual woman that was utterly at his mercy.

He had to confess that he wasn't paying all that much attention to the interview. Michael let Kendall's voice wash over him like a soothing melody, until something she said knocked him out of his fantasy.

"Children?" Kendall asked, looking at her interviewer, appearing faintly flustered for the first time in the show.

A hundred miles away from where Michael was, sitting on an uncomfortable couch in the middle of a studio set, Kendall was still reeling from the shock of being asked if she and Mr. Reese were planning on having children any time soon. She struggled to recover, and finally managed to answer with a shaky laugh.

"He hasn't even given me a ring yet."

However, the journalist was persistent. "But you wouldn't say no, Miss Bailey?"

"To the ring or the children?" Kendall wasn't sure if she could keep up with the jokes. It felt like she was slowly being cornered into saying something that could alter her life in a major way. She was hyper-aware that Michael would watch this and hear every word that she said. Of course, he would understand that she didn't have any control over the questions they asked, wouldn't he?

"To either, I would imagine," the interviewer shot back, leaning forward to give the impression of warmth and interest.

And so Kendall was forced to give the only answer that she could under the circumstances. She plastered a smile on her face, and replied slowly, "No. I wouldn't say no." She was extremely disconcerted when she realized that it was quite easy to give a true smile of happiness, getting caught up in the moment and the idea.

The remainder of the interview passed by without further incident. Kendall hardly remembered it. Her mind was still stuck on that question about children and marriage. She couldn't understand why it had thrown her so badly. There shouldn't be any doubts in her mind when it came to Michael and babies. Their relationship wasn't real. Still, there was no denying the appeal of a chubby little baby with Michael's velvet brown eyes and thick glossy hair.

Kendall's cell rang, providing a welcome distraction from her thoughts until she saw who was calling. "Hello, Michael?"

"Hi beautiful. I was watching you."

"Were you?" Kendall bantered back, glancing around at the bustle going on around her and slightly disappointed that she wasn't alone. "Where are you?" she asked, having forgotten his exact schedule for the day. Those weren't the kinds of details that Michael liked to keep her up-to-date on.

"In bed. I wish you were here with me," he chuckled wickedly, managing to bring a flush to Kendall's skin.

"Michael!" she hissed, but he only laughed.

"We could be working on those babies that you say you wanted," he continued playfully.

"You know I only said that because I had to!" She didn't have to admit the part where it felt really good to say it out loud.

MICHAEL KNEW that they couldn't carry on like this forever, but he didn't expect to be caught so soon. Their luck ran out just a couple of days before Michael was due to head back to Louisville. He was in New York a day later than planned, and Kendall was in the city too. She had come to give a speech on women's rights. Michael originally thought that he was going to miss her (and was annoyed with Thomas for making sure their schedules were slightly out of sync), but somehow, he had managed to catch a break. They both had a hole in their schedules at roughly the same time and he had the perfect opportunity to see her and recharge his batteries.

"Do you mind if we take a little detour?" Michael asked his driver through the plate glass window that separated him from the front of the car. "Miss Bailey should be finishing up her event. I think we have time to drive her to the airport. Kendall and I need to...discuss some strategy."

"Yes, sir," Bruno said. Michael chose to ignore the

knowing smirk on the other man's face and gave directions to the University where Kendall was delivering her speech. They arrived just as the event was ending, and he sat patiently in the limousine while Bruno went to fetch Kendall.

He was alone just long enough to stoke his already overexcited libido before the car door swung open and Kendall's face appeared.

"Michael," she gasped with equal amounts of pleasure and disbelief.

"Come here!" He pulled her into the car and started kissing her before she even had a chance to speak.

His hands pushed under her skirt, leaving no doubts about his intentions. "Can I give you a ride to the airport?" he asked, the darkness in his eyes hinting at the double meaning.

It was reckless to indulge himself with so many people nearby, but Michael didn't stop to think about just how reckless until after he helped himself to Kendall's body. By that point, he didn't really care.

Kendall laid her head against Michael's shoulder and curled her arms around his neck, uncharacteristically kittenish and docile in the wake of their lovemaking. He stroked his fingers through her hair and was vaguely aware that the car was moving. Bruno was obviously following his instructions to drive them to the airport. The stolen rendezvous would be over soon, but he pushed that knowledge aside for the time being.

"I've needed to do that for so long," he groaned.

Kendall smiled against his chest and then tilted her head so that she could kiss his throat and the underside of his chin. "Me too," she said and then began to ease herself off his lap. Michael caught hold of her and held her where she was.

"I want to keep you with me," he murmured thickly.

"You know I can't stay," she whispered, pulling away from him again, and this time succeeding. "You know it would damage the campaign."

Michael frowned. "You don't want to stay with me?"

She opened her mouth to answer, but at that exact moment, the limo rolled to a stop. Whatever she meant to say was replaced by a squall of horror as she surveyed her rumpled clothes.

"You can relax," Michael reassured her, calmly buttoning and zipping his trousers. "No one knew I was coming. There shouldn't be anyone here to meet us."

Oh, how very wrong he was.

14

*K*endall was a celebrity in her own right now, and the Press was eagerly awaiting her arrival. The second that Michael and Kendall stepped out of the car at the airport, they were caught in an explosion of camera flashes. Kendall pressed against Michael trying to hide her flushed and disheveled appearance. Thirty seconds of frantically smoothing down her skirt and patting her hair had done absolutely nothing to camouflage the fact that she had just been thoroughly ravished. And while let's face it, the American electorate was a lot less Puritanical than it used to be, she didn't know if they were going to be forgiving or meet them armed with metaphorical pitchforks.

Kendall glanced to Michael, wondering how on earth he was going to fix this mess. She didn't know if he was truly confident, or just exceptionally good at faking it, but he appeared unrattled. He reached for her left hand, held onto it tightly, and then turned to the shouting reporters with a dazzling smile.

"Well, obviously we didn't know you guys were going

to be here to meet us," he acknowledged with a boyish shrug. There were a few laughs, and several more questions yelled at him. "We were planning to tell our families the good news first, but seeing as you guys are here now, it will save us the trouble of arranging a press conference in a few days," Michael continued cryptically.

Everyone's attention, including Kendall's, was riveted on Michael, waiting for what he was going to say next. "Miss Bailey...Kendall and I are-" he paused and shot a heart-stopping smile down at her "-we're getting married."

Kendall's heart lurched as she heard Michael make the announcement. What was he doing? How could he do this without discussing it with her first? It's just a distraction...She told herself as she tried to control her reaction. No one was looking at her wrinkled skirt and unkempt hair now. The cameras were fixed on her left hand. There were a few cheers, and then cries of, "kiss her then, Michael!" and "show us your ring, Kendall!" filled the air.

Michael kept a tight hold on Kendall's hand, denying the paparazzi the shot they were craving. He paused for a few photographs, and then he practically dragged Kendall after him through the private aviation terminal. His bodyguards kept the reporter outside.

"What the *HELL* was that about?!"

Kendall and Michael both turned to see Tom standing just inside the doorway looking pale and irate. Kendall had forgotten that he planned to join her for the flight back to Kentucky. She had never seen the campaign manager so furious, and she couldn't deny that he was justified.

"I think we need to talk. Somewhere private,"

Michael said, his voice so cold and silky that Kendall shivered.

Michael, Thomas, and Kendall walked through to a small lounge at the back of the terminal in silence.

"Well?" Tom demanded the second that the door closed behind them. "Would you like to tell me what the hell you're playing at, Michael?"

"What I'm playing at?" Michael echoed icily. "Why don't you tell me what you're playing at, Thomas? I assume it was you who organized for those reporters to be waiting to mob Kendall without checking with us first?"

Tom's jowly cheeks went a nasty shade of red. "What's your point, Michael?" he growled.

"My point," said Michael slowly, "is that you are not in charge of this campaign."

Thomas flushed even darker. "Well, if that's how you feel, maybe you should start looking for a new campaign manager!" he bellowed, and then stormed out of the room.

It took a few minutes before the tension leaked out of Michael's shoulders, and he turned back to Kendall. "I guess this means we need to find you a ring," he said as if the scene with Thomas never happened.

"But- Tom!"

"Will calm down," Michael sighed. "He's a good man, a good friend, but we clash occasionally. It will blow over."

"And if it doesn't blow over?"

"I'd rather know I have to find a new campaign manager now rather than later."

"Michael, this is fucking insane," Kendall said.

"What are you talking about? What would you have had me do?"

"I don't know, talk to me about it first," Kendall said, her hands planted firmly on her hips to let him know she meant business. Just because she agreed to this, in the beginning, didn't mean that people could change the rules midgame and not discuss it with her. She liked Michael. A lot. More than she should and that was part of the problem. She couldn't let herself get sucked in and be left with nothing in the end.

Michael halfheartedly apologized but followed up again with nonsense about having no other choice. "Besides, I would do it all again in a heartbeat," he said to Kendall in a teasing tone and smiling wickedly.

"Even though we got caught?"

"Especially because we got caught. Surely, I'm allowed to keep my fiancé with me a lot more than my girlfriend?"

"So this was all just a plan to be able to sleep with me more often?" Kendall was cut off when Michael changed the conversation.

"We need to go out and get you a ring." He glanced at his watch and frowned. "I haven't got time to go out now; I need to check into my hotel, and then I'm due to meet up with some people for dinner."

"And I have to go back to Kentucky." She got the feeling that he thought she was going to stay here with him. The way he frowned when she pointed out that she wasn't confirmed it.

"But I want you to stay here with me," Michael pouted, kissing her neck hungrily, before moving his mouth back to her lips.

Kendall gave herself to the hot, drugging kiss, but she knew that it couldn't continue. She had to go, and even if Michael had stopped thinking with his brain, she wasn't going to let him cause any more trouble for the campaign by keeping her around.

"Think of your approval ratings!" she gasped disentangling herself from his arms.

"I'll have my driver take you to the airport if that's what you want?" he said at length.

Kendall nodded her head and tried to ignore the disappointment when he relented.

"I'll be back in Kentucky in a few days. The campaign trip will be over. And then we're going to go and find you a ring."

15

*M*ichael didn't like to think too hard about why he wanted to keep Kendall close. She had such a strange effect on him. He wanted to believe that it was just about the sex. It was lonely on the campaign trail, after all, and he was a man with needs, but he had a niggling feeling that it was more than that. He caught himself storing away jokes and pieces of news to tell her when they met again, thinking of places that he wanted to show her, foods that he wanted her to taste, even though he knew that their time together would run out long before he had a chance to follow through.

Fortunately, Tom returned to take Michael's mind off Kendall. As predicted, the other man was waiting in Michael's hotel suite later that evening. The campaign manager reminded Michael of a loyal dog that had just been kicked and beaten. Both men muttered apologies, and then they got on with the work that was still waiting to be done.

Michael's "engagement" to Kendall was the top story,

and it was all anyone seemed to want to talk about for the last few days of the campaign trip.

The Vance Campaign naturally claimed that the timing of the Reese-Bailey engagement was a cynical attempt to impact Michael's approval ratings, but no one guessed how close they were to the truth. Even his opponents seemed to accept that the relationship itself was 100% genuine.

Perhaps that was the problem, Michael mused, as he flew back to Louisville. Perhaps he was starting to believe the lie too?

He shifted uneasily in his seat and loosened his tie. It was hard to keep track of exactly what his real relationship with Kendall was. How much of what they did together was an act and how much of it was genuine? It certainly felt real when she was in his arms. Michael could charm just about any woman, but most couldn't hold his attention past the evening. Kendall was different. She was a sexy, intelligent woman whom he just happened to lust after around the clock... what did that say? He had to keep his eye on the prize. Winning this election was the goal, not marriage to Kendall.

Michael rubbed a hand across his eyes. He was too tired to think straight. It would all look clearer after a good night's sleep. A good night's sleep in his own bed. The thought alone was heavenly. Now, to make it truly perfect, he just needed...

"Stop it!" he growled at himself.

"Hmm? What? Where?" Tom grunted, waking himself up. He had been dozing in the seat next to Michael and quickly settled back down again when Michael didn't say anything else.

"Fuck," Michael swore, careful to keep his voice lowered this time.

This was a nightmare. He was trying to become the next President of the United States of America. He couldn't afford distractions; however luscious and lovely they might be.

It was all well and good telling himself that, but the whole country thought he was engaged to Kendall now. There was no way to undo what was already done. Michael had to figure out a better coping mechanism for being around her all the time.

Kendall was waiting for him in Louisville when he arrived hours later. She looked a little flushed and uncertain when she saw him and was greeted with a chaste peck on the cheek.

"I didn't know whether I should come or not... and then I thought that, well- if you were my real fiancé I would be here, so I came. Are you upset?"

"Upset?" Michael frowned, "Why would I be upset?"

Kendall shrugged and followed him toward the waiting car. "You just- you seem different."

"Different, how?" Michael pushed, even though he knew exactly what she was talking about. He was trying to create a distance between them that hadn't been there before. He already hated it, but he was not about to fall in love with this woman.

"I couldn't sleep on the plane," he said, yawning as if he was trying to prove it. "We haven't stopped for days. Isn't that right, Tom?" he called but was answered only with a gentle snore from the front of the car. "See?" he chuckled.

Kendall smiled. "You and Tom made up, it seems."

"We did, we always do."

Kendall nodded, and then she fell silent again. Michael didn't push her to make conversation. He was truly exhausted, and he was still trying to figure out exactly how he felt about his speech writer "fiancé." He was unnerved to find that simply being with her brought him pleasure. It was annoying.

He leaned back in his seat and watched her through half-closed eyes. She took his breath away every time he saw her. He didn't understand how she had been working for him for several months, and he never realized that she was gorgeous. It was a miracle no one else had snapped her up.

They dropped Thomas off at his house first, and then Michael surprised himself by asking if Kendall was coming home with him. The words were out of his mouth before he'd even had a chance to think of them. It seemed that he really couldn't control himself when she was near.

"I will if you want me to come with you?" she said, feeling a little more uncertain around him than the last time they were together. "I was under the impression that you wanted to be on your own."

"No!" Michael barked, and before he had stopped to think she was in his arms. "How can you say that?" he whispered, stroking his fingers over her face. Instead of answering, Kendall inclined her head slightly and brushed her lips against his mouth.

The shivers always caught Kendall by surprise. She would have thought by now that they would have stopped. Or she would be used to it by now. That wasn't the case, and every time Michael kissed her it felt like the first time. She wrapped her arms around his neck and nestled against him, all concerns over how distant he'd been momentarily disappeared. Before she could completely get her fill of him, Michael pulled back a little.

"Easy," he whispered, glancing towards the front of the car where the driver was sitting.

"Seriously, now you're shy? After last time?" she teased, reminding him of the last time they made love in a car. They ended up engaged." Kendall attempted to move and put some space between them, but Michael followed her.

"Point taken," he murmured kissing the tip of her nose. He glanced out of the window. "We're almost home."

"Home?" Kendall frowned, also looking out of the window; she wasn't anywhere near her neighborhood.

"You are coming home with me, aren't you?"

"Do you really think that's a good idea?"

"We're engaged. That's the beauty of the lie. What can anyone possibly say about you coming over to have dinner at my place?"

"I guess you're right." Kendall leaned her head on his shoulder. Michael eased his arm around her and held her close. It was such a nice feeling, being pressed up against his body like this. Comfortable and easy.

The car drove through nearly deserted streets. When Kendall looked out the window, she was surprised to see them turning onto Bardstown Road near her own house. She had never asked Michael where he lived but always imagined him in a gleaming high-rise apartment near the Riverfront. Instead, the car turned down a side street toward Cherokee Triangle.

The car drove through the gates of a grey-stone house with a wrap-around porch and lush lawn.

"Beautiful," Kendall said, sweeping her eyes up to the

slate roof, taking in the details. "Seems like a lot of space for just you."

Michael didn't answer, but he followed Kendall's gaze. He thought back to the first time that he had seen the house. He was still on his first marriage at the time, ecstatic to receive his first civilian paycheck. His defense contractor salary seemed borderline obscene after twenty years in the Army, and he had been so proud of the house, so full of ideas for filling it with children and memories.

Kendall noticed Michael's darkened expression and didn't say anything else. She followed him into the house, through a great foyer and into the kitchen, where he made a beeline for the fridge. A casserole was sitting on the top shelf of the otherwise empty appliance.

"I swear, Mrs. Martin forgets that I'm not her son sometimes," he said, looking amused, but not disappointed with his spoils.

"Mrs. Martin?"

"My housekeeper," Michael explained, popping the edible treasure into the microwave while Kendall dryly observed that all grown men liked to be mothered on occasion. Michael held up his hands in mock surrender. "Guilty as charged."

Michael poured a glass of red wine for Kendall and then helped himself to a beer from the fridge. He set out some plates and cutlery, pausing to cover his mouth as he yawned.

"Sit down!" Kendall instructed taking command.

"But you're my guest," Michael argued, but obeyed, sinking down onto one of the kitchen stools. "

"Just sit down and let me take care of you, Mr. Reese," Kendall said flashing him a flirty smile.

"That sounds promising."

Kendall laughed. "I don't think you're good for much more than eating your dinner and collapsing into bed tonight."

"Just as long as you collapse into bed with me."

Kendal smiled at his persistence, popping a quick kiss on his cheek before she collected the casserole from the microwave and dished it onto their plates. She felt like a retro housewife, cooking Michael his dinner at home after he had had a long hard day at work. There was nothing sexual about it, nothing even romantic, but it still left a lovely glowing warmth burning in the center of Kendall's chest.

They chatted about the campaign over the meal, about how Michael's trip had gone and what was still left to do.

"I still need to buy you an engagement ring," Michael said. "I thought about having Tom sort it out, but-" he ground to a halt, as though he had said something that he shouldn't have. He cleared his throat self-consciously. "Well, you should pick it out. You have to wear it, and Tom has dreadful taste."

"Don't you think we should go together?" she suggested. Picking out a ring together, the thought was both amazing and frightening all at the same time. She knew she was getting in over her head, but she couldn't stop the train now that it'd left the station, nor did she really want to.

Michael had finished his casserole. Kendall rinsed their dishes in the sink and then returned to the table.

"Come on," Kendall said, gently prodding Michael to his feet when he started to fall asleep in his chair. "Let's get you upstairs. You'll feel like a new man after a good night's rest."

"I hope so," Michael said and obediently followed her out of the kitchen. He took the lead when they got upstairs because obviously, Kendall didn't know her way around. "I promise to give you a full tour tomorrow morning after we sleep. It's this way," he said through another yawn, leading her towards the master suite.

"Are you sure you don't want me to go?" Kendall asked one last time.

He turned and stared down at her, his answer clear on his face.

endall awoke the next morning to the sound of the vacuum cleaner. She sat bolt upright in bed when she registered the sound. Beside her, Michael was still sleeping peacefully. She shook his shoulder until he opened his eyes. "Someone's here!" she hissed

"It's just Mrs. Martin," he shrugged, rubbing a hand over his eyes.

"Just Mrs. Martin?" she scoffed. "Michael! She can't know that I slept here last night! No one can know!"

Michael pushed himself up into a sitting position. He was frowning as he watched Kendall scurry out of bed and start to pull her clothes on. "I'm sure we can trust her not to run immediately to the press."

Kendall glared at him and continued to get ready. It turned out, however, that it wasn't Michael's housekeeper who they had to worry about.

Michael's telephone began to buzz. He picked it up and hit the answer button with annoyance. He hadn't even put it to his ear before he heard Thomas's irate voice bellowing down the line. It was so loud that Kendall could hear part of what Tom was shouting from halfway across the room.

Michael cleared his throat and hoped that he sounded calm and innocent when he spoke. "I'm sorry, Tom, I didn't quite catch that. Do you think you could lower your voice a few decibels and repeat what you just said?"

"Are you *trying* to ruin this campaign?" Thomas barked savagely. "What were you thinking letting Miss Bailey stay the night at your house?" he demanded, injecting each word with a burst of incredulous anger.

"Should I assume that one of the tabloids found out?" Michael sighed, running a hand through his hair.

"Assume that they *all* did, Michael," Tom spat. "And not just the tabloids either. You and Miss Bailey made one of the top stories on several TV stations this morning too."

"Fuck," Michael swore, cursing under his breath. He glanced at Kendall, who, if it was possible, seemed to have grown even paler.

"Quite," Tom said dryly, dragging Michael's attention away from his lover. "I took the liberty of making a statement on your behalf. I know you dislike my inference, but I thought-"

"Tom, just tell me what you said!" Michael snapped, losing a little of that hard-won composure that he had been struggling so hard to hang onto since picking up the phone.

"I said that you and Miss Bailey slept in separate rooms, naturally. I also said that she had stayed for purely practical reasons- you were fine tuning a speech together late into the night so it just made more sense."

"And did anyone buy that?" Michael asked doubtfully.

"I think we need to push the wedding forward," Tom replied, which told Michael everything he needed to know.

"Tom... I think you forget that there isn't meant to be a wedding," Michael pointed out, a little desperately.

HE WAS PREPARED to do anything it took to win the election- but marry Kendall to gain a few more votes? He didn't want to think about why that idea didn't have him running for the hills. The voters knew what they were getting with him. This wasn't the eighteenth century, and other Presidents had done far, far worse. It wasn't fair that he had to live up to Puritanical standards, but it was one of the terms Tom made him agree to when he signed up to be his campaign manager.

"Obviously I'm aware of that, Michael," Tom sighed. "But we have to at least seem like we're getting ready. This wouldn't be such an issue if it weren't for your reputation."

"All right," Michael growled, unwilling to sit through another lecture on his playboy reputation. "But-"

"We'll have Kendall jilt you just before the big day. Maybe she could leave you standing at the altar? I wonder how that would affect approval ratings?"

Michael hung up the phone without further comment.

Kendall was hovering near the side of the bed. She took a deep breath and stood up straight. "Let me have it. Is it terrible?"

Michael was still digesting everything that Thomas had told him, but he gave his head a wary shake. "We'll work it out."

"We will?" Kendall asked. "How?"

Michael told her Thomas's plan. "See, so all you need to do is jilt me at the altar, and everything will be back to normal."

"You want me to jilt you at the altar?" she repeated, looking decidedly unimpressed with the idea.

Michael allowed himself a cheeky grin. "Why not? You'd rather go ahead and marry me?"

"No! Of course not. That's not what I meant!" Kendall said quickly, but her cheeks were tinged with crimson. "If I leave you standing at the altar, you come away smelling like roses- the poor, wronged man thrown over by some wicked woman...but what happens to me?" she demanded. "I'll get ripped apart."

She had a valid point. "I'm sure people will forget about it pretty quickly," he murmured feebly.

"I'm sure they won't!"

"Well, what do you suggest we do?" Michael asked, rather harshly. "Because I don't see that we have too many options to choose from. Besides, you could always get a job working for the opposition. They'd love you for jilting me. Especially if it works out to their benefit."

Kendall glared at him. "Don't talk to me like that, Michael! This isn't my fault you know! I-!," but she stopped when she realized that her purse was ringing.

"You going to get that?" Michael muttered, getting out of bed while Kendall searched for her cell phone.

"It's my mom," Kendall squeaked, staring at her phone's display for a minute before plucking up the courage to answer.

Michael paused on his way to the bathroom to listen to Kendall's half of the conversation. She didn't seem to be getting many words in. Most of the time she was silent, and looked like she was getting the lecture of her life.

"No... *no*! I- yes... *yes,* Mom. No! He- yes, I know that, but-" she sighed heavily. "No, Mom, okay... yeah, I love you too. Bye, Mom."

"Problems?" Michael asked when the call was over.

Kendall shrugged helplessly. "Mom wants me to go home," she said weakly.

"You're not going, are you?"

"No, of course not. I know I can't go anywhere," she snapped.

"But you want to go?" It was selfish of him, but he had never really stopped to consider what an impact Kendall's relationship with him was having on her real life.

"No... I don't want to go," she said slowly. "I just-" she paused. "I just didn't think things would turn out like this when we started this lie," she mumbled.

"That makes two of us, sweetheart," Michael smiled sadly. "Look, I'm going to have a quick shower, and then we'll go down to breakfast together?"

Kendall nodded her head unhappily. "I don't think I want to venture out and meet your housekeeper on my own."

"Kendall, it's going to be okay," Michael promised, before disappearing off into the bathroom.

Easy for him to say.

17

"*M*aybe you can leave *me,*" Kendall suggested the second that Michael emerged from the bathroom. He had a towel knotted casually around his waist, and rivulets of water trickled through the hair on his chest. It took a lot of effort for Kendall to rip her gaze away. Once she managed it, she started studying her fingernails.

"Pardon?" Michael blinked.

Kendall knew it was a futile hope, but she proposed it again anyway. "Can't you leave me?" she said weakly. "You could jilt me. Maybe you decide that I won't make a good First Lady, or-?"

"Sweetheart, I think that would defeat the purpose of the exercise," Michael said gently. "Besides, you're probably going to enjoy jilting me. Especially after everything I've put you through. Think of it as revenge." His tone was joking, but Kendall found it a struggle to muster a smile.

Michael dressed quickly while Kendall tried to fix her hair. There wasn't much she could do to straighten it, and she had no choice but to wear her clothes from the night before. She followed Michael downstairs to breakfast when he was ready, not particularly eager to meet his housekeeper for the first time while performing a walk of shame.

If Mrs. Martin thought there was anything strange about seeing her employer stroll into the kitchen followed with a disheveled young woman, then she kept those thoughts to herself. Breakfast was already laid out on the table. Two places were set. Mrs. Martin exchanged a few pleasant words with Michael as he and Kendall sat down, and then bustled off into one of the other rooms to clean.

"So, I've been thinking," Michael said, helping himself to a strong cup of coffee. "We should go out this morning and buy you your engagement ring."

"Oh?" Without realizing it, Kendall's eyes went straight to her naked left ring finger

"I don't have anything planned this morning. I was going to give myself a day off to rest after the campaign, but I want to get a ring on your finger as soon as possible," he said simply.

Kendall wondered if she imagined the possessive edge to his voice. The ring was meant to stop the negative gossip and put a positive spin on the story, making it all feel more genuine. It wouldn't mean anything, not to Michael anyway. It was strange how one moment it felt like there was a connection that went beyond physical and then the second she got comfortable with him, he'd shut down and do something to remind her that this was all just a hoax. They were doing a good job of pulling it off too. Even her mother was fooled. Well, her mother was fooled into thinking she was in trouble, which she *was*, just not in the way that everyone imagined.

The chauffeur drove them on to Louisville's most exclusive jeweler. Michael's bodyguards walked them to the door of the store to save them from being mobbed. Kendall felt self-conscious. This really wasn't how any woman dreamed about getting an engagement ring.

The shop manager had been alerted ahead of time of their arrival and rushed over to help as soon as he saw them. Michael smiled at the man and said they were fine just browsing on their own for a minute.

"Well?" Michael turned to Kendall.

He looked awfully pleased with himself. She couldn't work out why. Did he actually think this was going to be a fun experience for her? A fake engagement ring? For all she cared, the diamond could be fake just like their relationship.

"Do you see anything you like?" he asked, looking at the glittering rings in the display cabinets.

She gave her shoulders a helpless shrug; she just wanted to get something and go. After a quick scan from several feet away she pointed to a case and declared, "That one's fine." She happened to point to one of the simplest, most inexpensive sets of rings in the store.

Michael frowned as he walked closer for a better inspection. "You can hardly even see the stone. There's no way my fiancé is going to settle for that ring!" he declared, reaching for her hand and maneuvering her towards the more dazzling choices.

"What about that one?" Michael asked, pointing out one diamond-encrusted ring that had caught his eye.

Kendall looked to see what he was showing her and promptly choked in her surprise. "Michael that ring costs-" but she couldn't bring herself to say the price out loud. "I really don't need anything so big." The first time anyone mentioned the possibility of an engagement at some point, she imagined an elegant, expensive ring like the one Michael was showing her. Imagining it in her head as a fantasy and standing in front of the real thing, preparing for a fake engagement was entirely different. It wasn't glamorous. It wasn't even fun.

Instead of being pleased by her reluctance to spend his money, Michael looked disappointed. "But I want you to have something nice," he insisted. "You deserve it."

"All of these rings are nice," she lied, and in truth, nothing had jumped out at her as being 'the one' yet anyway. Not even any of the more expensive pieces. "Besides. We're just going to return it anyway. A piece of costume jewelry would work just as well."

"We aren't going to return the ring!" Michael said with a ferocity that made her heart skip a beat. A tiny bubble of hope rose in her chest, but it was popped an instant later when he continued, "Consider it part of your compensation for helping out. You can sell it when all this is over, so that's even more incentive to pick out a really big one."

Michael didn't seem to notice that he was making her even *less* enthusiastic. Still, it was obvious that she would have no peace until she picked out a diamond that met his standards. "There. That one's fine," she said, picking out another band with a single stone. This one was only slightly bigger than the first one she had chosen.

Michael stared at her incredulously for a moment before turning away to beckon the manager over. "Excuse me." The man appeared almost instantly at Michael's side. "I was wondering if you had a private selection of engagement rings that you could show my fiancé? We seem to be having difficulty selecting a ring."

"Oh yes, of course!" gushed the manager. "Why don't the two of you take a seat other there and I'll bring over some options I think you'll be most pleased with?" he enthused.

"Michael!" Kendall said urgently," I don't think-!"

"That would be wonderful," Michael said, speaking to the salesman and ignoring Kendall's objection completely. He wrapped an arm around her waist and swept her towards the chairs that the manager had directed them to.

"What are you doing?"

"Forcing you to choose a half decent ring," Michael said smugly. Kendall couldn't stop herself from glaring at him. "I told you. I want you to have something nice." Almost as an afterthought, but not quite, he added, "Besides, if you don't have a stunning ring everyone's going to be calling me a cheapskate."

Again, it was all about his image. "Oh, I see," Kendall sniffed, hating the crushing weight of disappointment that she felt. It did make her consider picking out the most expensive ring the store had to offer though.

"Now, perhaps the lady would like one of these rings?" said the store manager, coming over and presenting Kendall with diamonds of different shapes and sizes. She didn't have to fake her gasp of delight. Her dream ring was sitting in the middle of the tray.

"Which one?" Michael smiled. He had been watching closely for her reaction.

Kendall pointed to a platinum band with a large round center stone surrounded by a halo of smaller diamonds arranged roughly in the form of a snowflake. It was breathtaking. "That one," she breathed reverently.

"Oh! An excellent choice!" gushed the manager.

"Do you want to try it on?" Michael asked, grinning broadly. Kendall nodded her head eagerly, and the manager helped slip it onto her finger.

"It fits perfectly!" Kendall gasped, moving her hand from side to side so that she could admire how the diamonds sparkled in the light.

"Must be fate," Michael chuckled. He popped a gentle kiss on Kendall's lips, catching her by surprise, before turning back to the manager. "We'll take it," he nodded.

The other man looked like Michael had just made his day.

"You didn't even ask what it cost," Kendall said in a rough whisper.

"Sweetheart, if you have to ask the price then you can't afford it," he winked, leaving Kendall to continue admiring her ring while he got up to sort out payment and insurance with the manager.

Kendall stared down at her left hand. It felt so strange to be wearing a ring on her fourth finger- strange and slightly wonderful. She sighed sadly and finally confessed to herself the thing that she had been trying so hard to deny: that she would have been happy with one of the smaller rings if it had meant that their engagement was real. Despite her best intentions, she had fallen hard.

"You ready to go now, Kendall?" Michael asked, reappearing at her side. "I thought we could go out and grab some lunch if all this shopping has made you hungry?"

"Do you think that's a good idea? With all the press and everything?" Kendall asked doubtfully. "Maybe-maybe we should do our own thing for a bit?" she suggested.

Michael frowned at her, and Kendall felt a touch guilty. He had just spent a small fortune on her after all.

"Do you want to spend some time apart?" he asked slowly. "I mean, is this too much, am I crowding you?" he frowned.

"What? No!" Kendall said quickly. "It's just-"

"That being endlessly hounded by photographers and reporters isn't all it's cracked up to be?" he smiled dryly, finally realizing she was rejecting him. She was rejecting the attention that came along with spending time with him.

Kendall flushed. "Well, do we really want to give them something else to write about?" she asked doubtfully. "Don't you want them to focus on your politics? Not your love life? You've got to get them back on message."

Michael was fighting a frown as he and Kendall stepped outside. He didn't want one of the photographers to catch him coming out of the jewelers looking unhappy, but he couldn't help feeling like a little black raincloud had just settled over his head.

"Ideally yes," he said, after thinking over Kendall's question for a couple of minutes. "But I can't help remembering that the whole reason we find ourselves in this... unusual position... is because Tom decided that my politics and love life couldn't be separated."

"Well, yes that's true," Kendall nodded, dragging her eyes away from her hand so that she could look up into Michael's face. She flushed guiltily. "I'm afraid I don't know how helpful I've actually been in that respect," she said, giving him a twisted smile that made her look neither happy nor sad. Just pensive. "I don't know if you wouldn't have been better off simply staying single."

"I have to be honest with you. This is not the way I

thought this day was going to go. This is the first time I've given a girl a ring, and she turns around and sounds like she's trying to break up with me," Michael said gently, trying to make it seem like he was joking. Truth was, he was unable to account for the heavyweight that was suddenly hanging around his heart.

Kendall smiled again, and then looked innocently back at her hand. "No, that's not what I'm doing at all," she said, admiring her ring. "Besides, it's not like there haven't been one or two benefits for me along the way."

"Is that so?" Michael grinned, thinking of the 'benefits' that he had enjoyed. It took him a moment to get his mind back on track. "So, lunch or no lunch?" he asked, unwilling to admit to himself how much her answer meant to him.

"Oh, what the hell. Lunch I suppose!" Kendall laughed, not catching Michael's sigh of relief.

18

*M*ichael spent the rest of the day working to get his politics back to the forefront of everyone's minds. It wasn't going to be easy. Tom sent over a selection of the morning headlines: "**DE-BRIEFED!**" blared one, over a blurry picture of Kendall leaving Michael's house. "**Reese concentrates on 'Fun'-Raising After Rally in Chicago**" proclaimed another. "**Kentucky Candidate Hard-On the Campaign Tail!**"

"Keep it classy, internet," Michael muttered under his breath before moving the links to the trash and trying to concentrate on the education initiative they planned to roll out the following week.

"How do you get yourself into these messes, Michael?" he muttered clicking the window closed and returning to his work.

Kendall woke up asking exactly the same question the following morning. She laid in bed feeling queasy for a quarter of an hour before a terrifying thought crept into her head.

"Oh my God!" she cried, sitting up in shock, and immediately regretting doing anything quickly. She clapped a hand over her mouth and breathed deeply through her nose until a wave of nausea had passed and then did some quick addition on her fingers.

She was late.

She eased her legs out over the side of the bed and reached for her purse. She rooted through the contents until she found her phone, and then pulled up a calendar app. Another tap brought up the screen that showed when she had her last period.

Only a few days overdue. Kendall tried to calm herself. She had been under an incredible amount of stress this past month, after all, and she was never completely regular to begin with.

Despite her best efforts, the quiet voice of reason was no match for the frisson of panic that was rising in her chest. She and Michael hadn't used any protection. She hadn't even thought about it.

"It must have been something I ate," the voice in Kendall's head continued to lobby for calm, "I'll stop at a drugstore on the way into work and get a test. That will put my mind at ease."

"*Unless the test is positive,*" the panicked side of her psyche chimed in, and she felt like throwing up again.

How could she have been so stupid? Kendall chastised herself. She never, ever took these kinds of risks. Getting caught up in the moment was no excuse but she was such an idiot where Michael was concerned.

The fact that she was still feeling queasy an hour

later, when the driver arrived to take her to work, did not bode well.

It had to be a mild case of food poisoning or simply a bug that was going around. Kendall continued to console herself as they drove downtown. It was way too soon for morning sickness anyway.

Despite her efforts to stay calm, Kendall couldn't stop her mind from spinning out of control. What if she was pregnant? It would ruin Michael and destroy his chances of becoming President. How was she even going to tell him? The idea was terrifying.

"Can you stop over there at the drug store please?" Kendall blurted to her driver. She couldn't wait a second longer to find out if her life was about to take a drastic curve.

Ten minutes later, she returned to the car with a pregnancy test hidden away in her bag. She was careful to make sure that no one saw her buying it. After the news coverage her sleepover had garnered, she didn't want to think about what the gossip sites would say if they found out.

Kendall's stomach did a funny little flip flop every time she thought about Michael. To be honest, the thought of having his baby wasn't wholly repulsive. She felt the same as she had when they were buying the engagement ring. She glanced down at her hand and sighed sadly. If only it was real. She was a fool for feeling that way, but she couldn't help it. Somewhere along the line she had fallen for Michael Reese. That wasn't part of the plan.

Seeing Michael at the staff meeting that morning was torture for Kendall, especially with the pregnancy test sitting in her purse like a ticking time bomb. She tried to be as inconspicuous as possible, but Michael's kept seeking her out and smiling secretively. He really did put on a good show of pretending that they were in love.

Kendall wanted to take the test straight away, but she was still trying to keep up with her own work, as well as her First Lady engagements and there was a stack of urgent messages sitting in her inbox. Once she started working, she was swiftly engrossed. It was lunchtime before she even had a chance to pause and catch her breath. Kendall was just about to run out for a bite to eat when she heard a knock on her office door.

"Come in," she said.

"Hey beautiful!" Michael called from the doorway. "I wanted to stop and see you before we head out. I'm going to Dallas after I-"

He was interrupted by Kendall's phone.

"I need to take this," she said, apologetically.

Michael nodded to indicate that he would wait.

He sat down on a chair in front of Kendall's desk, accidentally kicking her purse over as he did so. Kendall was absorbed in her call and didn't pay any attention as he reached down to clean up the mess.

Michael picked up Kendall's wallet and her house keys, and then he reached for a rectangular box that had also tumbled out onto the floor. His fingers wrapped around it before he realized what "it" was. Michael froze for at least ten seconds as he stared in horror at the pregnancy tester kit in his hands. He glanced up at Kendall and was glad to see she was completely ignoring him while on her call. It gave him a moment to jam everything back into her purse.

Michael sat back in his seat, trying to come up with any logical explanation for why Kendall would have a pregnancy test that didn't end with her being pregnant. Perhaps he misread the box, or maybe Kendall picked it up for a friend? Anything was possible. Only, none of those explanations was the most likely. She probably had a test because she thought she might be pregnant. Kendall might be having his baby. That thought sent another jolt shooting through Michael's body.

Kendall might be carrying his child.

Michael wanted children, but a family had always been something he promised himself 'one day' and in recent years that day looked like it would never come. He had accepted that.

"Did you want something?" Kendall asked, breaking his mind out of the dark clouds by smiling at him. She had finished her telephone conversation and Michael hadn't even noticed.

"I-" What did he want? He barely remembered. "I... just wanted to say goodbye before we fly to Texas.". His mind continued to go a million miles a second. Should he confront Kendall with what he had seen, or should he wait for her to mention it? He wasn't sure that he could handle the conversation right now. He felt completely knocked for a loop and needed to get a grip on the situation.

"Are you feeling okay?" Kendall frowned, staring at him anxiously. "You look a little pale. You aren't coming down with something are you?"

Michael shook his head. "I'm fine," he said automatically. "A bit tired I guess."

She gave her head a sympathetic nod but the look on her face said she didn't quite believe him. "You have to pace yourself, Michael. You don't want to burn out. Where would the campaign be then?"

Oh God, the campaign!

Michael rubbed a hand over his face. If Kendall was pregnant then his dreams of becoming President were over. No one was going to elect a man who had knocked up his girlfriend. It would be different if Kendall was his wife.

That was it. That was the answer. He had to get the wedding pushed forward.

"Michael? *Michael!*" Kendall's worried voice sliced through Michael's thoughts and dragged him back to the present.

"Sorry," he apologized, smiling weakly. "Must have zoned out for a minute."

Kendall examined him closely. "Are you sure you're not sick? I was feeling a little under the weather this morning. Maybe there's something going around?" She sounded strangely hopeful.

"I don't think so," Michael said slowly. He tried to collect himself. "You were feeling unwell this morning?"

"Yes, but it passed," Kendall said curtly. "So- you're leaving for the airport straight away?" she asked, changing the subject so abruptly that Michael couldn't fail to notice what she was doing, especially when he knew why she was doing it.

He grunted an affirmative reply and then fell into contemplative silence. This was going to be a press nightmare for both of them. Michael realized something though. In between the thoughts of worry and dread, he felt a very tiny, very delicate bubble of excitement. He imagined that if he focused on that small feeling and allowed it to take hold it would grow into more positive feelings towards Kendall's pregnancy.

Kendall seemed like the kind of woman who would

make an excellent mother. Michael managed to summon a smile when he thought about Kendall totting a little baby around on her hip. *His baby*. Something primitive and masculine inside him approved strongly of that idea. Besides, if the voters wanted a First Lady, surely a whole family would be even better? Maybe he could make this work.

Yes. They simply had to get married. Michael's smile grew. He couldn't help himself. Now that he was obligated to marry Kendall, he could admit to himself that the idea held a lot of appeal. He liked her a lot. He lusted after her around the clock, and now she was carrying his baby. What other woman would make half such a suitable wife...and First Lady?

Michael wasn't ready to give up his presidential dreams just yet. He just had to get Kendall down the aisle as soon as possible, before there was any speculation about her condition. Once they were married no one would care about a pregnancy. The election would be over long before the baby arrived, and then they could spin some story about the baby being premature.

"You look a little more cheerful?" Kendall remarked, noting the rapid change in his expression.

"I am. I've reached a decision," Michael said cryptically. He leaned back in his chair and pressed his fingers together thoughtfully.

"Oh? That's... good?" Kendall frowned. "A decision about the campaign?"

"In a way..." Michael nodded, speaking slowly. It was probably better if he didn't mention anything to Kendall about pushing the wedding forward just yet. He was bound to phrase it wrong. He couldn't let her think he was only marrying her because of the baby. Women got so silly about practical reasons like that. He would have to convince her that it was for the good of the campaign to move their wedding forward. Then, once things were underway for their 'sham' ceremony, it would be easier to convince her that they had to go through with it. At least, he hoped that was the case.

19

*N*egative. It was *negative*. She wasn't pregnant.

Kendall sat down on the edge of her bed, stared blankly at the pregnancy test in her hand and tried to summon up the relief that she knew she ought to be feeling.

"This is good," she said aloud, as though she was attempting to convince herself. What was wrong with her? Kendall looked up and stared in disgust at her reflection in the mirror on the dressing table.

She was hardly past her prime, but still, she didn't have years to dally if she wanted to raise a little family of her own. Perhaps she had secretly seen Michael as a solution to that problem? Not wittingly of course. Maybe, subconsciously there was something in that theory?

When a woman was thinking about her baby's genes, she could do a lot worse than Michael Reese.

A pregnancy would have been a disaster. There was no two ways about it. Wanting to have a baby with a man she didn't even have a real relationship with was idiotic. That was even without the whole 'President' angle.

"I've got to be more careful," she murmured, resolving to get back on the pill as soon as possible. Michael wasn't exactly the careful type, so it was up to her to make sure that there weren't any more potential accidents.

Sighing, Kendall threw away the test and its box, taking care to bury it beneath a layer of discarded papers and banana peels.

She was halfway through revisions on the speech she was working up when her phone buzzed. Michael's number was on the screen.

"Hello? Michael?"

"Hey, Kendall." His voice was oddly strained. "I thought I'd call to see how you're doing. So, how are you doing?"

"I'm... fine," Kendall answered, trying not to think about the drama that had just unfolded in her bathroom. "Why? Is something wrong?"

Kendall knew that Michael flew to Texas immediately after their lunch. His campaign appearances were scheduled so tightly that she didn't expect to hear from him at all until at least the following morning when he got back to Louisville. She wasn't complaining. She loved the fact that he had called her for no other reason than to see how she was, apparently, but she was curious.

"I just-" Michael cleared his throat. Kendall couldn't remember ever hearing him sound uncertain before. It was unnerving.

"How are *you* doing?" she demanded, baffled by his behavior. "Is something the matter with the campaign?"

"Not exactly, but I do think that we need to change our plans," he said,

"What plans?"

"Our wedding plans."

Michael held his breath and waited to see what sort of a response his statement would provoke from Kendall. She was silent for a few seconds, before echoing his words.

"Our wedding plans? What do you mean? What kind of 'changes' do you want to make?"

Michael cleared his throat again. I want it to be real, he thought to himself, but couldn't yet make that confession aloud. "I think we should move the ceremony forward," he blurted, wondering if this might help prompt Kendall to make a revelation of her own.

It didn't.

"Move the date of the wedding forward? What for?"

Thankfully, Michael had come up with an excuse to explain away his suggestion if Kendall didn't mention the baby on her own. He was hurt and slightly annoyed that she hadn't told him yet, but he was determined not to show it.

"I just think we need to be concentrating solely on the campaign when we get closer to the election date," he said easily. It wasn't a foolproof explanation, but he hoped that Kendall would buy it.

"I... see?" Kendall said doubtfully.

"Do you?"

"Yes, of course. You want me out of the way sooner rather than later." Kendall's voice was flat and expressionless. Michael couldn't tell what she was really thinking- or feeling, for that matter.

"That's not what I mean," he said quickly. He couldn't quite manage to match Kendall's control; this was the mother of his child he was talking to, of course he didn't want her out of the way. What he wanted was to marry her.

"Well, I don't see how else to interpret what you're saying. I'm not angry," Kendall added quickly. "It's better if people elect you knowing that you won't have a real First Lady. Some of them are going to be really pissed off if they find that out only after you're elected President." She added a small, humorless laugh to the end of her sentence.

Michael scowled on his end of the telephone. How could he tell Kendall that the rules had changed? He didn't want a sham engagement any longer. He didn't want to be jilted at the altar. He wanted Kendall to be his wife. He wanted them to bring up their child together.

"Michael? Are you still there?"

"I'm here," he murmured. *Why couldn't she just tell him that she was pregnant*, he wondered bitterly. Surely, she knew him well enough to know that he would do the right thing by her? "I'm going to talk to Tom about all of the arrangements that need to be changed," he added slowly. Surely Tom would be on his side? The campaign manager would see the sense in making Kendall marry him as soon as possible.

"It's going to be okay, Kendall," Michael blurted, wanting her to realize that things had changed, that he knew what was wrong, and was willing to take care of both her and their child. *Their child*. Something warm and powerful spread through Michael's body, starting in the center of his chest and moving outward. He was going to be a father.

It was completely impossible for him to be thinking about anything else. He couldn't even concentrate properly on the campaign. He just wished that Kendall would come clean about the baby so that he could be excited about it all out in the open.

"Michael? Are you still there?" Kendall asked after a long pause.

"Yes. Sorry. I'm here," said Michael quickly. He had to stop letting his thoughts wander.

"It's getting late, and I have to be up early tomorrow," Kendall said.

Michael glanced at his watch. It wasn't that late, but he had read somewhere that expectant mothers were tired all the time.

"Okay, well I'll let you go then. Take care of yourself, Kendall," he added huskily before saying goodbye.

Kendall put down the phone and stared at the receiver with a puzzled frown. There was no denying it, Michael had sounded off. Nothing like his usual, confident self. He was distant and distracted. Maybe he was bored with their arrangement? That would explain why he wanted the sham wedding pushed forward.

Kendall worked a little bit longer on the speech before heading home for a microwaved dinner and bed. She felt weak and battered, even though she now knew that there was nothing physically wrong. Maybe that was the problem? It had given her a guilty thrill to imagine carrying Michael's baby.

Now it seemed that he was in a hurry to disentangle himself from her completely. She knew that this day was coming. She tried to prepare for it, but her heart had been having problems since the very beginning of their phony relationship.

It was all just sex and politics to Michael though. Kendall didn't have a clue how she was going to be able to keep working for him once things were over. Was she even going to be allowed to stay?

She hadn't asked Michael what was going to happen

to her after their public breakup. If she was going to jilt him, there was no way he could keep her on his staff.

"Damn," she whispered. Kendall was disgusted with herself for becoming so swept away by passion and not realizing the threat to her career. Her professional reputation was already suffering from the perception that she had slept her way into the job. Things could only get worse after a high-profile ejection from a Presidential campaign. It wasn't like speech writing jobs were plentiful. Her position was precarious to say the least.

Kendall didn't think that Michael would treat her unfairly. He would probably help her find a new job, or at least pay her off handsomely for her troubles. She scrunched up her nose in disgust at the latter idea. It made her feel dirty. She didn't want his money unless she had no other choice. Why hadn't these consequences occurred to her before?

"Because you're an idiot!" Kendall growled at herself.

She should never have agreed to any of this.

20

"What do you mean, you want the wedding pushed forward?" Tom asked, frowning at Michael.

"I mean just what I said, Tom. I want the wedding pushed forward."

"Why?" the campaign manager demanded suspiciously. "Miss Bailey is a huge hit with the voters and we already have campaign events booked with her through the end of October. You can't possibly be bored with her already. Can you?"

"Of course not," Michael growled, hoping that the heat he felt rising to his face wasn't showing. He couldn't imagine ever becoming bored with Kendall.

"Well then, I don't see any reason to change our plans. The closer the breakup happens to the election, the greater the public sense of sympathy will be when they go to vote," Tom pointed out sensibly. "Or we could even wait until after the election, but before the Inauguration, of course. We could say that the pressure of becoming First Lady was too much for her- "

Michael winced, and wondered how he was going to admit to Tom that there would be no public sympathy to count on? The other man hadn't finished speaking, though.

"Besides, if you rush into the marriage, or are perceived to rush into the marriage, you know very well what the media will say. Especially after your little slumber party last week."

"I do?" Michael muttered, but he knew exactly what Tom was driving at.

"Of course, you do. They'll all be saying that you've got her into trouble," he snorted. "And by the time it becomes apparent that she isn't, the damage will already be done."

Michael cleared his throat awkwardly and loosened his tie. Tom watched the uncomfortable behavior for a moment and then paled. He sat down opposite Michael.

"She's not-?" Tom croaked. "You haven't? You wouldn't be that stupid?"

Michael shrugged his shoulders and managed a sheepish smile. "It was an accident."

Tom couldn't find his voice for several seconds. "You're an accident! An accident that's been waiting to happen. Oh my God, this is-" he groaned, rubbing his temples and shaking his head. "Well, you know what she's going to have to do, don't you?"

"Marry me?"

"Fuck no!" Tom swore. "She's got to get rid of it."

Michael blinked, and stared dumbly at the other man, convinced that he must have misheard, until Tom started naming clinics where the proposed abortion could take place.

"Kendall can have an abortion over my dead body!" Michael snarled viciously.

Tom looked up at him in amazement. "Michael, think about what you're saying," he implored. "Your political career will be over if anyone finds out about this."

"Not if we're married," Michael retorted, his face thunderous.

"People can count Michael!"

"I don't care what you say, Thomas, some things are just more important than winning elections."

"I- I can't believe what I'm hearing," Tom stuttered. "We've been working toward this campaign for eight years. You have hundreds of people counting on you, millions of voters looking to you to improve their lives, and you're willing to throw it away for some girl you've barely known for two months? You aren't being rational. What does Miss Bailey say?"

Michael opened his mouth, but promptly shut it again, unwilling to admit that Kendall hadn't even confessed to the pregnancy yet, much less discussed how they would proceed.

"Kendall agrees with me."

Tom shook his head. "If she had any sense at all she would have dealt with the matter before telling you," he muttered under his breath.

Michael wondered if Tom knew how close he was to getting a broken nose.

21

The following afternoon Kendall was back in her office, still trying to catch up on work. She read over the speech that she had prepared for Michael's address to the Youth Education Foundation and allowed herself a satisfied smile. It wasn't easy keeping up with her writing in snatches of stolen time between fundraising dinners and making her own appearances, but she had met her deadline. It was good work, too. Possibly some of her best. She was inspired by what she had seen on the campaign trail. Michael Reese wasn't the only one that had managed to touch her heart. The people that she had met as she travelled across the country had intrigued and challenged her. She understood why Michael was working so hard.

She had just finished an e-mail to the campaign communications director when there was a tap on her office door.

"Come in?" Kendall smiled uncertainly when Michael's campaign manager came barreling into the room. "Hello, Tom, is there something I can do for you?"

"Yes! No! I don't know-" he said wildly.

Kendall arched a brow. She didn't think she had ever seen the man in such a state before.

"Is something wrong?" she asked, standing up from her chair as he charged into the room. She was confused when he glared at her accusingly.

"As if you don't know, Ms. Kendall," he said sarcastically, and you could see the man struggling not to roll his eyes. "I came here to tell you, but perhaps it's not my place, and Michael will be furious," he said, now muttering practically to himself. "But if I don't say anything..." He continued like that for several moments before reaching some sort of conclusion. "You do realize that this is going to kill his career?"

"What's going to kill whose career?" Kendall demanded, confused.

"Oh please, what do you think I'm talking about?" Tom spat. "Your pregnancy of course!"

"My... my what?" Kendall choked and sank back down into her seat as the words hit her in the chest, taking her breath away. It took her a moment to regain her composure.

"Don't pretend you don't know what I'm talking about. Michael's told me everything."

Kendall just blinked at Tom. Michael told him? Why did he think she was pregnant? This didn't make any sense. She had a scare, but there was no way for Michael to know that.

Kendall licked her lips. "Tom, calm down and tell me exactly what Michael said to you."

"That he intends to let you keep the baby. Can you imagine?" Tom snorted. "He said that he's going to marry you."

Kendall couldn't believe her ears. It was lucky that she was sitting down, because she really would have fallen this time if she hadn't been. Michael would have married her, really married her? Only for the baby, she reminded herself.

There wasn't any baby, of course. What would that mean to Michael? Surely, he would be relieved? Obviously, the intention of marrying her sprang from his sense of duty and a desire to limit damage to his campaign. He really was willing to do just about anything to get an opportunity to lead this country.

She had to tell him the truth. Immediately. Or did she? For just a second, Kendall wondered what would happen if she did nothing. What if she let Michael continue to believe that she was carrying his child? Kendall pushed aside that dangerous thought almost as quickly as it had occurred to her. She was a little bit ashamed of herself for even thinking it.

"I..." she started to speak, but then faltered. Should she tell Tom the truth too, or keep it between herself and Michael? Tom was involved enough, she decided. "I'll talk to Michael."

"Good, you make him see sense," he grunted. "I don't say it isn't a sad business, but." Tom didn't bother to finish his sentence.

"I know, I know, it would ruin Michael's presidential campaign. Have you given a single thought to my feelings and what this would do to my life?" Kendall interrupted Tom before he could say anything else to infuriate her.

He was momentarily stunned and at a loss for words.

"Never mind," Kendall sighed, letting him off the hook way too easily.

Tom glanced at his watch. "Well, if you go now Michael should be free to see you."

Kendall sighed again and got to her feet. Tom was really pushing his luck. "I suppose I'll be on my way then." Mentally she added, *you ass.*

Tom stepped back to let her pass through the door. Barely aware of the path she took to get to Michael's office, Kendall found herself in front of the door before she knew it. She'd been too preoccupied with trying to work out what on earth she was going to say.

She tapped lightly on Michael's office door, secretly hoping the he would be out or too busy working to see her. She had no such luck. Michael's voice immediately called for her to enter. When she stepped inside, she saw that he was alone.

"Kendall!" Michael smiled, getting to his feet when he saw her standing in the doorway. He walked around and dabbed an affectionate kiss on her forehead. "We just got back a few minutes ago. What's up?"

She licked her lips as she considered her words. "Thomas just came to see me." She was looking down at her feet, so she didn't see the furious way his eyes flashed.

"Oh, he did, did he?"

"He said that he spoke to you."

"Whatever he said, it doesn't matter," Michael hissed. "I assume he told you that I know about the baby? Well, I don't care what else he said, because I'm not going to let anything happen to either of you."

It was a surprise to hear him admit his knowledge on the baby so freely and without anger. In that moment, Kendall wished so hard that the pregnancy test had been positive.

"Oh Michael," she whispered, blinking back guilty

tears. She had no choice but to immediately come clean. This had to stop right here. "There is no baby." She wasn't able to meet his eyes as she broke the news. She heard him sit down in the large leather chair behind his desk. When she summoned the resolve to look up, she could see that he was shaken.

"But I saw it," he started, then stopped. He shook his head and frowned. "You wouldn't lie to me about this would you?" he demanded. "Tom hasn't convinced you to get rid of the baby without telling me?"

"As if I'd let Tom have any real influence on whether or not I'd keep a baby." Kendall answered, unable to believe that Michael had really asked her that question. "I'm not pregnant," she insisted. "I never was. Why would you think that?"

Michael was staring down at his hands. "I saw the test in your purse and made the obvious assumption," he said quietly. He was still frowning suspiciously. "Why did you have the test, anyway?"

"Because I thought...well, we haven't exactly been careful, and I was feeling a bit under the weather."

Michael seemed to know what she was trying to say without Kendall having to find the exact words.

"You must have been relieved when you found out that you weren't pregnant," Michael said bitterly.

"No," she whispered, as tears strung the backs of her eyes. "No. I wanted to have your baby," she confessed, but then immediately clapped a hand over her mouth in horror at what she had just confessed.

"Did you really?"

"I shouldn't have said that," Kendall said hurriedly.

"Shouldn't you?" Michael questioned, his eyes were bright with question. "Didn't you mean it?"

Kendall couldn't bring herself to lie to Michael, even though she sensed that would have been the wiser decision. The timing wouldn't have been ideal, but the truth was, she had wanted to have his child. Something about Michael made her reckless.

He urged her backward, until she was pinned between his body and the door. "Maybe I wanted to make you pregnant," he growled, which made Kendall gasp and burn.

Michael lowered his lips to her mouth, stealing a savage kiss as he pressed their bodies together.

"Stop! I can't think," Kendall gasped, trying to pull away from him, but she was denied. Michael captured her mouth again, plunging his tongue between the seam of her lips and drinking his fill of her.

"I don't want you to think," he panted. "Tell me what you feel?" he rasped, letting his hands wander hungrily over her body.

"Michael, no," Kendall whimpered half-heartedly. She couldn't stop herself from returning his kisses, and her arms had wound automatically around his neck. "We shouldn't," she puffed, but only because she was certain that Michael would ignore her.

"I want to be inside you," he growled, nipping at her neck. Kendall shuddered and moaned. "I want you to have my baby."

"Oh God," Kendall groaned. Was it possible for a man to say anything more arousing? Every rational thought that she possessed had fled in the face of Michael's overwhelming desire.

"Tell me you want it too," he urged, grinding against her shamelessly.

"I do!" she sobbed. "I do!"

A tiny part of Michael was still hanging onto reality by a thread. He had to stop. Kendall didn't know what she was saying. He didn't know what he was doing. These thoughts flashed through Michael's mind, but not one of them was powerful enough to still his hands or lessen the passion of his lips.

Somehow, dimly, he knew that thread of control he was hanging onto just slipped from his grasp. Michael couldn't put into words the crushing disappointment that had broken the bonds of his restraint, but it was tearing him apart. Kendall wasn't pregnant. There was no baby. He should have been relieved, but all he could think about was his failure as a man. Even though he hadn't been trying, it still somehow felt like a defeat.

He wanted her pregnant, damn it. He wanted to see her swollen with the seed of his child. He wanted the world to know that she belonged to him.

"Michael!" Kendall gasped, as he continued with increasing roughness to paw her body. "Easy, baby" she said, breathless, but her plea went unheeded and the sensual sound of her voice only seemed to urge him on.

Michael reached around her to fix the lock on the door, while his other hand continued its groping caresses. "I need to be inside you," he growled.

Kendall whimpered as Michael lifted her completely off the floor and pushed her back onto his desk, scattering his papers everywhere.

She couldn't restrain the moan as Michael tore at her stockings and panties, and pushed up her skirt.

He didn't make any apology to her for his almost violent treatment; he was acting on instinct alone. He could sense how badly she wanted him too.

"Please?" Kendall begged, clutching at Michael as he

took a brief step back from the desk. He moved away from her so that he had room to reach for his belt and free the throbbing rod of his sex.

"Soon," Michael promised, groaning thickly.

"Now," she begged.

"*Now,*" Michael agreed raggedly, tipping his hips and entering Kendall in one smooth, sure thrust.

"Oh!" she gasped, clinging to him frantically, and rolling her bottom forward to force him even deeper into her body.

Michael grunted and tightened his hold on her. It always felt incredible to be held inside Kendall's body, but there was something different this time. Something extra raw and frenzied. He should stop... he shouldn't be taking her like this, not here, but Michael couldn't help himself.

He knotted his fingers in Kendall's hair and forced her to tilt her head back. It was a better angle so that he could claim her mouth in a savage kiss as he continued to piston inside her. She, in turn, wrapped her legs around him, urging him faster. Deeper. Harder.

"Fuck!" Michael swore, nearing his peek. "Oh fuck!"

"Don't. Not yet," Kendall sobbed, but a second later they both froze when suddenly there was a knock at Michael's office door.

It would have been comical had it not been so terrifying that Kendall's eyes nearly popped out of her head. She tried to scramble away from Michael, but he refused to let her go. He kept her exactly where she was, impaled upon his twitching shaft and hushing her with his eyes.

"Michael!" she hissed, trying to speak and stop him without physically making a sound. He shifted his weight so that he could glance over his shoulder, knocking against the inside of her sheath in the most provoking manner as he did so. Kendall bit back a moan as illicit pleasure sizzled through her veins.

Her excitement was only intensified by the fear of getting caught, it appeared, because when the knock on the door was repeated more loudly than before, and she felt Michael throb inside her and she too sighed with pleasure. She did give her head a frantic shake when Michael withdrew and then thrust powerfully between her legs.

"The door's locked," he mouthed silently, quickly finding a steady, almost silent, rhythm that was pushing Kendall higher and higher every time their bodies reconnected.

"Michael!" she pleaded, her voice a mere whisper. Fortunately, it was drowned out by a much louder shout of Michael's name. Tom's voice called through the door from the hallway outside. The door handle rattled, and a new clutch of fear made Kendall's muscles contract tightly around Michael's cock.

"That's my girl," Michael murmured thickly, burying his sex between her legs with renewed vigor. He claimed her mouth, swallowing the cries that she was incapable of suppressing as her whole body shattered dizzyingly, fluttering and pulsing, and bringing Michael to his own devastating climax.

Kendall went limp in Michael's arms as he spilled his seed against her womb; her orgasm had left her kittenish and weak, but as its dizzying effects slowly faded away reality started to come crashing back down around her. What in the world had they just done?

"I didn't..." Michael started to say but frowned and shook his head. "No, I did mean to do that," he growled unapologetically.

Kendall shivered at the bold statement; there was something unforgivably sexy about it, what they had just done.

"I know I shouldn't have, though," he added bleakly.

Michael's gaze dropped to Kendall's stomach. She saw where he was looking and flushed. "I don't really think," she started to say, but Michael cut in before she could finish.

"I'll take full responsibility if you are."

"You don't have to say that," she said as she gingerly pushed herself off the desk.

"Damn it, Kendall, I'm trying to...," Michael growled, but he stopped himself when the knocking at the door resumed. "Oh, for the love of God!" He straightened his clothes and then started towards the door.

"Michael!" Kendall gasped. She glanced down at her own disheveled appearance and knew that she would never be able to fool the person at the door into thinking that she looked anything but thoroughly shagged.

Acting completely on instinct, she darted into the bathroom adjoining Michael's office and shut herself inside while Michael answered the door.

"What is it, Thomas?" Michael barked at his campaign manager.

The other man looked startled by this rough, sudden address. "I was, well, I was just passing by, and..." but then he frowned and glanced into the office behind Michael. "I sent Miss Bailey to see you. I thought perhaps she might be here?"

"I know you sent Miss Bailey to see me," Michael said, unable to forget his fury with the other man for interfering in his private affairs. All right, so there was no baby now, but Michael still couldn't forgive Thomas for his behavior and for what he had wanted done if there had been a child.

"And?" Thomas asked casually.

"And we've... sorted things out," Michael said, trying to sound casual. He glanced quickly about the office for Kendall, as Tom forced himself inside.

Michael was relieved that Kendall was hidden. He really didn't think that he was feeling up to yet another lecture from his campaign manager.

"How have you sorted things out, Michael?" Tom demanded shrewdly. He gave a delicate, curious little sniff, but didn't comment on the earthy scent that was hanging in the air. Or maybe he smelled her perfume. "Has Miss Bailey managed to talk some sense into you?"

Michael didn't think that he would have explained what had happened between himself and Kendall in those bland terms but agreeing with Tom seemed like the quickest way to get rid of him.

"She did," he said blandly.

"Well... good," Tom nodded, but he didn't look entirely convinced. "So everything is back on track? We'll keep the wedding at its original date. Miss Bailey will jilt you, and then everything can go back to normal. Thank God."

Michael heard the weary tone of Tom's voice. "This was your idea," he couldn't resist pointing out. "You were the one who said I couldn't do without a First Lady by my side."

"Well to be honest I think we might have been better off leaving you single and toning down your playboy image."

There was a time when Michael would have agreed with this sentiment whole-heartedly, but he wasn't sure now if he would change the circumstances that had brought Kendall into his life. If only he hadn't been so blind where she was concerned. She had been working for him for months, why couldn't he have discovered her delights on his own? Then, all the little misunderstandings could have been avoided. "Well, it's too late for that now. We'll have to go through with things as we originally arranged."

"Right," Tom nodded. "I'm glad to hear that we finally agree. Remember, I know a doctor who can help out if need be."

"That won't be necessary," Michael grunted.

"But Michael!"

"Leave it, Tom," Michael said, a note of warning in his voice. "Trust me, I know how to handle this situation."

"All right, well, I'll leave you to it then," Tom said slowly. He sniffed the air again and frowned at the papers he had just noticed lying on the floor. "Ugh, here," he said, pulling a piece of paper out of his pocket. "Those are the numbers you said you wanted."

"Thanks, Tom," Michael muttered, pocketing the paper as his campaign manager made a hasty retreat out of the office. Once he had been gone for a safe amount of time Michael called out to Kendall. "You can come out now. He's gone."

The bathroom door creaked open. Kendall was still delectably rumpled when she stepped back into the room.

"You didn't have to hide you know," Michael said. "It might have taught Thomas a lesson if he had found us together."

"It's probably better that we didn't. I don't think Tom

163

can handle any more surprises," Kendall said with forced cheerfulness. "In any event, it sounds like we're back to the original plan of me leaving you at the altar?"

"So it would seem," he murmured slowly. "Unless you have a better idea?"

Kendall opened her mouth, but no sound came out. How could she possibly reply to such a question? She could never admit the truth, that what she really wanted was for them to get married for real. She had already confessed to wanting his baby in the heat of the moment. It was a ludicrous idea, of course. They hardly even knew one another. Why did everything have to feel so impossibly right with Michael?

"No. I don't," Kendall said eventually.

"Me either," Michael sighed, dragging a hand through his hair, mussing it even more than it had been mussed to begin with. Kendall was sure that she wasn't imagining the gleam of regret in his eyes, and it gave her a small sliver of hope.

he next few weeks seemed to slip into a weird, hyper-accelerated state of time. The days flew past. Everyone involved in the campaign was rushed off their feet. No one was more harried than Michael of course, but Kendall was a very close second. She was still writing Michael's speeches and prepping him for debates, making appearances as a would-be First Lady, and planning a wedding that would never happen.

Kendall initially assumed that Tom would take the lead in planning the ill-fated ceremony, but he refused to be involved. She supposed it would give the whole charade away if the campaign manager was dealing with caterers or ordering flowers.

Michael paid for a wedding coordinator, which was a relief, but there were still endless decisions to make. Kendall would not have minded handing over the reins to someone else. It wasn't an ideal way to plan a wedding, knowing that no one was going to enjoy the day. People were taking time out of their busy schedules to attend a sham and the more Kendall thought about it, the harder it was to get excited about cake samples and bridesmaid dresses.

Kendall's mother was thrilled, if confused, by the whirlwind romance. Of all the people Kendall was lying to, this was the hardest, but she didn't know what else to do. Her mother wanted to meet Michael before the wedding. So far, Kendall had managed to put her off

By the end of September, the cumulative stress was starting to take its toll. It felt like a gray cloud was hovering over Kendall wherever she went, even when she stopped by Michael's house to go over a few speeches that she had prepared for him to use in the final weeks of the campaign.

Kendall had barely walked through the door when she received a text informing her that the candidate was caught in a last-minute meeting and wouldn't be home for hours. Kendall thought about heading back to her own house, but the prospect of seeing Michael was the only thing she had been looking forward to all day. She helped herself to a glass of wine and then curled up on the sofa to wait, passing the time by reviewing a few pages of polling data that was sitting on the coffee table.

The race was still too close to call, but Michael did have a tiny lead. Victory was within their grasp as long as they didn't get complacent.

One thing was certain, Michael wasn't slowing down his efforts in the slightest. A proud smile tugged at Kendall's lips when she thought of her fake fiancée. She didn't think that she had ever seen anyone work as hard as Michael had over the last few weeks. She was awed by his drive and passion. Most days he started off by meeting voters in blue-collar diners for breakfast, held press events until lunch, wolfed down a sandwich during strategy sessions at noon, then jetted off to all ends of the country for evening events and rallies. Even his weekends were packed. If Michael did catch a spare moment, he spent them canvassing door to door with his volunteers. To be honest, a tiny part of Kendall resented that he was gone so often. At the same time, his determination to win reminded her of what an incredible man he was.

"Kendall?" Michael's tired voice called through the house and Kendall set up with a start.

"I'm in the living room, Michael," Kendall uncurled her legs and got up off the sofa. "I didn't hear the car," she said apologetically, as her fiancé entered the room. "The office said you wouldn't be home until later? Do you want to order takeout for dinner?"

"Sure," Michael nodded. "Is Chinese okay with you? I don't think I can eat another pizza."

Kendall nodded and typed their usual order onto a telephone app, then texted to inform the secret service agents stationed outside that they were expecting a delivery. Michael sank down on to the couch, moving aside a stack of papers and magazines to make room for his long legs. He glanced at one of the glossy covers and read the title, *American Bride*.

"When is the big day?" he asked, although he knew the answer. "It must be getting pretty close now."

"The first Saturday in October," Kendall answered. "I forget the exact date."

Michael's eyes narrowed. He wondered if she was lying. He knew the exact date. It was only two weeks away. Two weeks really wasn't a very long time. It was only fourteen more days. That meant they had, at most, only thirteen more nights together. He dragged a hand over his face, unwilling, but unable to deny the misery that accompanied that thought.

"Food is on the way," Kendall said, finally looking up from the screen. She knew this wasn't the best time but since she was running out of opportunities, she decided to ask a question that had been bothering her. "Michael, about the wedding... what's going to happen exactly?"

Michael didn't feel like facing that discussion yet. Ever the politician, he avoided the question completely by occupying Kendall's mouth with a deep kiss.

He wasn't sure how he was going to be able to give this up, the luscious feel of Kendall in his arms and the luxury of being with a woman who saw him as just a man, not a public figure. He could be himself with Kendall. He didn't have that ability with anyone else. It was going to be so unbearably lonely without her.

Michael tugged Kendall down onto his lap, relieved when she melted into his embrace and didn't try to resist him or attempt to talk. His lips moved reverently over her soft, smooth skin, trying to tell her without words exactly what it was that she meant to him. *Everything.* But he wasn't ready to admit that yet.

Michael raked his fingers reverently over Kendall's body. It was going to be unbearable when she was gone. He had been lonely for years, but it would be so much worse now that he knew exactly what he was missing. He would only have memories to keep himself warm.

Michael ran his fingers lightly through Kendall's hair, lovingly curling the dark, silky tresses around his digits. *To hell with it all. Why couldn't they just get married for real?* Michael jolted at the thought. He wasn't sure what had given birth to that idea, but he found it impossible to dismiss.

Would it really be so crazy? Plenty of marriages were built on less than what he and Kendall shared. Didn't Michael's own history prove that was true? What he felt for Kendall was a hundred times more intense and more genuine than anything he had ever felt for either of his previous wives.

Michael toyed with the idea, wondering what Kendall would say if he suggested it out loud? Would she laugh at him, or worse, refuse him point blank? He couldn't guess. Michael knew, or thought that he knew, he meant something to Kendall. He just wasn't sure what that something was, or if it was as much as she meant to him.

He wasn't a coward though and when he wanted something, he went after it. Michael had never shirked away from any challenge in his life. He was just on the cusp of asking Kendall if she would marry him- for real- when Kendall's phone buzzed.

"Food's here!" Kendall gasped, leaping off Michael's lap and straightening her clothes.

Michael grunted, trying not to show his acute disappointment. He might not be a coward, but he wasn't sure if he would reach such an extreme level of recklessness again.

The doorbell rang and he forced himself away from Kendall's side. "I'll get it," he said. Kendall watched as he left the room. There was something different about her fiancé this evening. Michael was always attentive, but there seemed to be some extra layer of meaning to Michael's caresses that she hadn't been able to decipher.

If only she knew what it meant.

he final push toward the election began the following Monday. The first three days were such a hectic bustle of speeches and rallies that Michael and Kendall hardly got to exchange two words. There were moments when Michael was alone though. In those quiet moments, when he ought to have been thinking of strategies to win Iowa or plans to get out the vote, he found himself instead wondering what would happen if he lost the election. He and Kendall could be together then.

"Are you paying attention?" Tom muttered, snapping Michael out of one of these daydreams

Michael dragged his attention back to the present. They were attending one of the final and most important rallies of the entire race. A senator up for reelection was the first speaker. Her speech was winding down to a close.

Kendall was scheduled to go next. Michael tried to dampen the flutter of nervous excitement that pooled in the pit of his stomach. This was the first time that he and his fiancée had delivered remarks at the same event, so he had never seen her speak in person. He didn't know what she was going to say exactly, and he hated to admit how eager he was to find out. Of course, Kendall was only going to say what people wanted to hear, but somehow Michael believed that he would be able to read her face and pick out the truth from the lies.

He clapped politely as the senator wrapped things up and left the floor. Michael looked around, trying to spot Kendall before she walked out and took her place in the spotlight. His eyes caught hers just as she stepped out onto the stage.

Michael smiled at Kendall. He wanted to give her one last kiss for good luck. He wanted to tell her how proud he was of her. He wanted her to know how much it had meant to have her by his side- but of course, he couldn't. He could only watch along with everyone else.

Kendall looked out at the sea of faces in the rowdy crowd and fixed a smile on her lips. Then, she took a deep breath, and began to speak.

"I am so grateful to have this opportunity to stand in front of you all and say a few words about my fiancé, Michael Reese, and why I firmly believe that he should be the next President of the United States. Long before I fell in love with Michael, I was inspired by his long and dedicated career of service to the American people. I was so drawn to the energy and passion that he brought to his politics and campaigns that I decided to quit my old job and come to work for him if he would have me. Luckily enough, he decided that he would."

There was a small ripple of laugher, which Kendall paused to allow. She hoped that the ardent tone of her voice was doing its job convincing the party and the public of Michael's merits, and not making Michael question where such passion was coming from.

"You see, that's what Michael Reese is like," Kendall continued, "he makes people want to change. He makes them want to be better. He cares about people and causes, and he has the drive to get things done, because the people who work for him believe in him."

Michael tried to keep himself grounded and not to let Kendall's words touch him too

deeply. He kept listening to Kendall talk, but she had turned her attention to certain policies of his campaign, things that he had heard and spoken about many times before, and so he was momentarily more interested in replaying what Kendall had said about being in love with him. His attention was recaptured by Kendall's voice a few minutes later.

"...and what is more, Michael is a fighter! He earned his medals the old-fashioned way, by putting his life on the line for his country. No one will defend this nation or its ideals more vigorously or more selflessly than Michael Reese. He will always, *always* be first in the line of fire."

Michael grinned. What man wouldn't smile after a compliment like that? He hadn't really talked to Kendall about his life in the Army. He wondered if she had really researched his career or if she was just adding a rhetorical flourish to what she already knew.

He wondered which he preferred, but didn't get much time to dwell on it, because Kendall was wrapping up her speech, and it was almost time for him to join her on stage.

"...and so, now I ask you to join me in welcoming the next President of the United States, Mr. Michael Reese!"

Michael squared his shoulders and then stepped out to the thunder of applause that erupted after the would-be First Lady's speech. He walked up to Kendall, who was beaming and clapping harder than anyone else. Acting on impulse, he swept her into his arms and kissed her until she lost her breath.

Cameras flashed and people whooped, but during the few delicious seconds that their lips were locked, everything else faded into the background.

"Thank you," he whispered.

Kendall looked puzzled but didn't have a chance to ask what she was being thanked for before Michael walked past her to stand behind the podium.

Kendall stood next to him as he spoke. Michael became ever more aware that this was where she belonged: by his side.

The crowd roared as the candidate began his speech. He focused on their faces, trying to connect personally with as many people in the audience as possible as he explained to them why he deserved their vote.

Kendall was waiting when he left the stage.

"That was incredible," she said approvingly. "They loved you."

"You didn't do so bad yourself." He smiled, almost shyly. "I especially liked the part at the beginning."

"About the foreign policy?"

He laughed and dabbed another kiss on her cheek. "The part about 'before you fell in love with me'."

"That?" Kendall shot him an answering grin. "Travis Bart in the D.C. office wrote it for me. You don't think anyone knew that I was lying, do you? I mean, it sounded convincing, right?"

Michael felt the blood drain from his face. He didn't

really expect Kendall to repeat her declaration of love, but he also didn't expect her to claim it was a lie to his face.

"Michael?"

Belatedly, he realized that he hadn't answered her question. She was frowning at him.

"Did I say something wrong?"

"Of course not," he said tightly, refusing to meet her eyes. He saw Tom moving toward them and seized on his escape. "Can you give me a minute?"

Kendall nodded and stepped aside, allowing Mr. Winterson to take her place.

"Are you feeling okay?" the campaign manager said. "You're looking a little gray."

"I'm fine," Michael growled. "Just tired."

"Well, you were fantastic out on the stage. Kendall too. I have a reporter from the *Times* who wants to speak with both of you."

"Kendall can't," Michael spat.

Tom arched a brow.

"I mean...she needs to go. She has something that she needs to do for the wedding tomorrow. I'm not sure what it is, but she needs to get back to Louisville tonight. Can you manage that?"

"You don't want her to stay for the party?"

"I don't," Michael said, surprised that it wasn't a lie. He knew that it was petulant to send Kendall away, but he was still stinging from her rebuke. It was stupid for him to think, even for a moment, that Kendall's declaration of love had been anything other than a campaign ploy, but he still needed time to lick his wounds.

"I'll take care of it," Tom said quietly. When Tom spoke next, he had lowered his voice considerably. "We need to discuss exactly what's going to happen, Michael."

174

Michael groaned. It didn't take a genius to figure out what Tom wanted to talk about: the end of the affair. This would all be over soon. Was that a good thing, or not?

24

---

*K*endall stared out of the plane window. She couldn't see anything except her reflection in the glass, and that wasn't a particularly cheerful sight.

This is for the best, she told herself, trying not to read too much into Tom's insistence that she return home before the rest of the team. After her pregnancy scare, the campaign manager made a point of reminding her, as often as possible, that this was all pretend. Still, she couldn't shake a nagging feeling that Michael was angry with her for some reason. Yes, she should have done a better job vetting the speech before she gave it. It was common knowledge that she came to the Reese campaign after working for the other side of the aisle. Fact checkers on opposition blogs were probably full of derision about the easily disprovable lie that she joined Michael's campaign out of some sort of star-struck dedication to his policies, rather than making a calculated career move. It was just the sort of petty nothing-burger that they obsessed over, and she knew how much these easily avoidable blunders made Michael insane.

Maybe it was better this way, Kendall thought. If she weaned herself off Michael gradually maybe it wouldn't be so bad when the final break came? She didn't believe that though. She had a feeling that nothing would make it easy to say goodbye.

Kendall still wished that she could have stayed around for the afterparty. Unlike the fundraisers that she attended almost every night, this was a party just for the campaign team. It was a "thank you" from Michael for all of their hard work, a "deep breath" before the craziness of the wedding and the election scattered everyone across the country. Even if she hadn't been Michael's "fiancé", she was an important member of his team, and she deserved to be there celebrating with everyone else.

The days that led up to the wedding passed in a hazy blur. Sometimes Kendall felt like time was rushing by. Other times it seemed to have stopped dead. She thought about Michael more than was healthy, but she just couldn't stop herself. What else was there to think about anyway? She sent him one final speech, the one he would have to give after she had jilted him. Then, all she had left to do was wait.

Kendall's mother arrived the night before the wedding. There was no way to keep her from coming. Kendall wished that she didn't have to embroil her mom in the lie. The older woman was excited at the thought of having such a prominent public figure as her son-in-law. She was going to be disappointed.

Kendall tried to wear a smile on her face as she walked through the wedding rehearsal with her bridesmaids, but her mind was a million miles away. She couldn't stop thinking about the discreet black leather folder that Tom had slipped to her early in the evening. She didn't have to look inside to know what it contained: a passport, plane tickets to Europe and the address of a small house in the south of France where she was supposed to lay low until the election was over. Tom had already informed her of the arrangements. The terms were generous, but she couldn't take any pleasure in the thought of the all-expenses vacation. There was nowhere on Earth far enough away for her to forget what it was like in Michael's arms.

Despite her raging emotions, Kendall slept like a baby the night before the wedding. Her mother had to come into her bedroom to nudge her awake.

"Rise and shine," the older woman cooed happily. "You have a big day ahead of you!"

Kendall groaned, and tried to pull the covers back over her head, but her mother whipped them away and then produced a breakfast tray with bacon and eggs, as well as the homemade cinnamon rolls that Kendall loved as a little girl.

"Mom," she said, tearing up at the gesture.

"Oh, don't start. You'll make me cry too! This is going to be the happiest day of your life, Kendall, and one of the most tiring," her mother said with feeling. "You need to eat something now to keep your strength up. You probably won't get another bite to eat all day."

"I'm not hungry, Mom," Kendall said. In all honesty she felt rather sick. She didn't have a clue how she was going to get through the day. The thought of Michael waiting for her at the church and being humiliated in front of all those people was unbearable. The whole world would be watching.

"I know you're excited, but please just try a few bites? Then, you can jump in the shower. The hair and makeup people will be here at eleven."

Kendall watched her mother leave, and then glanced at the telephone that was sitting on her bedside table. Should she call Michael, just to check in and make sure that nothing had changed?

Kendall didn't realize that she was holding the phone in her hand until her mother reappeared and shrieked at her. "You're *not* calling Michael, are you?"

Kendall didn't know why her mother made that assumption. "I was only going to check on him."

The other woman snatched the telephone away. "That's almost as bad as seeing the groom before the wedding," she said. "We don't want any bad luck today, do we?"

"No, we certainly don't." Kendall managed a weak laugh. *Bad luck*. If only her mother knew what was coming.

Kendall's mother put down the telephone and looked at her daughter's untouched food. She sighed. "Well, if you're not going to eat anything you may as well get out of bed."

"I'm sorry, Mom," Kendall apologized suddenly. She was sorry for so much more than just ignoring the breakfast that had been made with pure love. A mom's love."

"Don't be silly, Kendall. It's only breakfast. Besides, I imagine most brides are too nervous to eat much this close to the wedding. Go and have your shower. I'll be back with your stylist in a little while."

Kendall nodded unhappily and slunk into the bathroom. She wished they hadn't decided to play out the jilting on the actual day of the wedding. It would have been almost as effective to break off the engagement the day, or even a week before. It would have been far less traumatic that way, although it would lack the same drama.

Kendall wasn't left alone for a single second after she emerged from the bathroom in a fluffy white robe. A whole team of aestheticians was waiting for her in the bedroom. There was someone to dress her, someone else to do her hair, someone for her nails, her makeup and various other forms of primping that she didn't quite understand.

Kendall had asked two of her sorority sisters, Ava and Maya, to serve as bridesmaids. She heard their voices over the thrum of hairdryers speculating with excitement about which celebrities might attend the reception. Little did they know they wouldn't have to do anything but ride to the church and back.

"Do you have your something borrowed, Kendall?" her mom asked, popping her head into the room where the girls were getting ready. I have your grandmother's brooch for the something old, and a little present for your something new..."

"You really don't need to bother," Kendall said dismissively.

"What's the matter with you today?" her mother demanded, concerned. "Don't you want your wedding day to be perfect?"

The older woman didn't wait for an answer. She was distracted by Kendall's wedding shoes, which were sitting on top of their box laid out on the dresser. She picked up one of the glittering white pumps and turned it over in her hands. "Oh!" she squealed happily, holding it up for the bridesmaids to see. "Something blue," she beamed, showing them the robin's egg blue soles.

Kendall rolled her eyes, drawing a hiss of annoyance from the woman who was trying to apply her mascara.

Kendall was quiet and obedient for the rest of the time that it took to get ready. Everything was starting to feel frighteningly real. When she finally looked in a full-length mirror and saw her reflection, she was literally dumbstruck for several seconds.

"I look like a real bride," she whispered once she found her voice again.

The remark was met with a chorus of laughter.

"Well, of course. What did you think you would look like?" her mother asked with a smile. "That's what you are. Now hurry and get your things. The photographer is going to be here any minute." With that, she exited the room, leaving Kendall to gaze at her reflection for a little longer.

"You look beautiful, Kendall," Maya gushed.

"Michael isn't going to know what's hit him," Ava agreed with a giggle.

Michael wasn't even going to get to see her, Kendall thought gloomily. She must have looked like she was on the verge of tears because both bridesmaids sprang forward with shouts of "Don't cry! You'll smudge!" which succeeded in drawing a half-amused smile to Kendall's lips.

"Are you all right?" Maya asked gently, frowning with concern. "You don't seem very happy."

"It's just last-minute nerves," Kendall shot back with a shaky laugh.

"Okay..." Maya said doubtfully and didn't manage

anymore because the photographer arrived and wanted to take a few pictures before they set off for the church.

Everything was spinning rapidly out of control. Before Kendall knew what was happening, she was in a limo with her bridesmaids and they were on their way downtown to the cathedral.

Ten minutes...

Tom had told her to wait until they were ten minutes into the drive and then tell the driver to turn around.

Fifteen minutes passed and Kendall said nothing.

"You're very quiet, Kendall," Maya said, frowning. "Is everything okay?"

"I can't," Kendall blurted, but the rest of the words stuck in her throat. She felt as though she was on a roller coaster that she couldn't get off. She didn't *want* to get off.

"You can't? You can't what? Have you changed your mind?" Ava asked and frowned.

"I can't," Kendall repeated and then paused. She took a deep and steadying breath. The plan was crazy.

There was only one thing that she could do.

$\mathcal{M}$ichael breathed out slowly and stole a glance at his watch. Kendall was late.

He smiled bitterly. Of course, she was late. *She wasn't coming.* Part of his brain, or maybe it was part of his heart, couldn't comprehend that fact. They hadn't had a real conversation since he sent her home from the rally, but avoidance had done nothing to dim his feelings. He was addicted, and he couldn't accept that she was really gone. He hated how distant they'd been. Just going through the motions made him realize just how much he didn't want to play pretend anymore. And now it was over. They never even said goodbye to each other.

Michael glanced over at Thomas, who mouthed 'wait five more minutes', and then he went back to staring straight ahead at the altar. A few moments later, he accidentally caught the eye of the priest. The old man nodded his head and flashed him a reassuring smile. Michael sighed heavily and shifted his weight from foot to foot. He couldn't believe how tense he was feeling. He started to crack his knuckles, until his best man softly cleared his throat, and Michael realized what he was doing. He stopped, just as he saw Tom slowly getting to his feet out of the corner of his eye. *Here we go*, he thought, as his heart sank into his stomach.

Michael nearly jumped out of his skin when the organ started to play the wedding march. He saw Tom freeze, halfway between sitting and standing, and then all the guests rose to their feet as the back doors of the cathedral swung open. Maybe he was still asleep? Maybe he hadn't really woken up that morning and this was all just part of a dream. It didn't feel like a dream though.

Michael craned his neck to look up the aisle. Someone hissed at him to turn around, but the second he saw Kendall he couldn't possibly have looked away. She was standing at the back of the church, clad in a sparkling confection of silk and lace, her dark hair peeking from behind a delicate veil. She was beautiful. She was everything that he had ever wanted and more. It was as if someone had peered into the secret hopes and desires of his heart and crafted a woman from what they found there.

The spell was broken, however, when Michael realized that Tom seemed to be having some sort of an attack in the pew behind him. His eyes bulged, and he gesticulated wildly with his hands. Michael shook his head sharply. He wasn't sure what Tom was trying to communicate, but he could only imagine that it was a plan to stop the wedding that was now in progress. Michael didn't know what the hell was going on, but he didn't want Thomas ruining it.

When Kendall drew by his side, Michael realized that she was shaking. He tried to smile at her but couldn't quite manage it. He was just too overawed. He couldn't believe she was there. Had she misunderstood her instructions? Was she going to run out on him in the middle of the ceremony? Michael honestly didn't have a clue, but, if there was a way for him to drag the marriage vows from Kendall's lips then he was determined to find it.

The Priest spoke, and Kendall stayed. The hymns were sung, and Kendall stayed. The marriage vows were started, and Kendall still stayed.

Michael stared down into her face, slowly beginning to trust that she was really going to stay until the end of ceremony. Then the Priest asked if there was anyone present who knew of any reason why they couldn't be joined together in holy matrimony. At that moment, Michael assumed that one of two things would happen: either Kendall would bolt, or Thomas would blow the whole thing.

Nothing happened though, nothing at all. There was blissful silence, and then the moment of terror was over.

Michael had been such a mess of fear, confusion and hope, that he hadn't paid much attention to what was said, but when the priest beamed and pronounced them husband and wife Michael knew exactly what to do. He covered Kendall's lips, bestowing a deep soul-stirring kiss that sealed the promises that they had just made to one another.

Mine, Michael thought to himself, as a deep wave of pure male satisfaction swept through his body. He didn't have a clue what had just happened, but Kendall was his wife now. She was wearing his ring. She belonged to him.

"Michael?" He heard Kendall croak, after they walked back out of the church hand in hand. She sounded as terrified as he had felt throughout the ceremony. Michael laid a possessive hand on the small of her back and kept her moving forwards. He was not ready to hear that she regretted what had happened or that it had been some huge mistake.

"Later," he whispered, hardly moving his lips. He fixed a broad smile on his lips. It wasn't that hard to maintain. He was genuinely happy with how things had turned out, and he was going to work extremely hard to make sure that Kendall stayed his wife. They could worry about just exactly how this miracle had come to pass later.

They didn't have an opportunity to speak alone. As soon as they were settled into the limo, they were whisked away for a photo shoot at Churchill Downs. Michael hadn't been aware of the crowds when he entered the church, he had been rather preoccupied, but he couldn't fail to see and hear them now. There were thousands of people outside cheering.

"Michael?" Kendall whispered. There was a desperate sort of urgency to her voice. "Tell me you're..."

"Smile," he interrupted, leaving the window down to smile and wave at the crowd as the cameras flashed.

There were more crowds waiting outside Churchill Downs. Security kept them all at bay, but he could hear them cheering as the wedding party posed inside the paddock and at various places on the grounds. They posed for more photographs than Michael could imagine that they would ever need, and then they climbed back into the waiting limousine and were finally accorded some privacy as they headed back downtown to the Brown for their reception.

Michael sank back into the comfortable leather car seat, trying to work out exactly what he wanted to say to Kendall, but he couldn't find any words. He stared at her, taking an extra few moments to work out what it was that he was feeling. Relief was one of the strongest emotions that he was experiencing. He thought that he'd lost her. Complete and utter confusion was also quite high on the list of things that he was feeling. Could they truly be married? It hardly seemed to be real.

"Say something." Kendall said. She was looking over at Michael with wide, uncertain eyes. He frowned when he realized that her back was practically pressed up against the door, ensuring that she was as far away from him as was physically possible.

"What would you like me to say?" he asked, dodging the question, wasting a prime opportunity to confess to Kendall how he really felt about her. He shuffled across the seat, reached for his wife and tugged her into his arms.

Michael's frown stayed exactly where it was when he didn't feel Kendall soften in his embrace. She was as rigid as an iron girder.

"I'm sorry. You must be so angry that I put you in that position," she said in a quiet voice trying not to cry. "I know I didn't follow the plan. I was going to...and then everything was happening so fast, and I, well, I just let it happen." Her self-control was admirable, but she couldn't prevent one crystal tear from sliding down her cheek.

"Aww, hell, Kendall," Michael swore roughly, searching his tuxedo for tissues or a handkerchief, anything that he could wave in her direction to prevent further tears. "Please don't cry?"

"I'm not crying," Kendall answered, but her voice was thick with the effort of maintaining control, "But...You married m-me. Why?"

Well, if that wasn't a verbal equivalent of a kick in the gut, he didn't know what was. It was a miserable thought. He cleared his throat. "You didn't want me to marry you?" he asked. "I thought-" but he suddenly didn't want to tell her what he had thought about her changing her mind, or about them being able to have a real marriage. "You came to the church. I don't see what else I was meant to do given the circumstances."

"I know, I don't know why but I couldn't."

Michael waited for Kendall to add something further, but she didn't. Instead she pressed the tissue he had offered against the rim of her eyes, trying to preserve her perfect makeup

Michael sighed heavily. A glance out of the window told him that they were almost at the hotel, and a glance at his wife told him that they weren't at all ready to get out of the car. He pressed the button for the intercom to talk to the driver and requested that they drive around the block again slowly.

Kendall managed to finally look at him when she heard that. Her cheeks had turned a delightful pink. "People will assume that we're up to something in here."

"I know," Michael smirked. Personally, he would rather people believe he was indulging in the wedding-night pre-party. It was better than the reality of seeing his wife's pale, unhappy face because they were married. "Dry your eyes," he said gently, trying to work out how he was going to turn this situation around into a positive.

Kendall was his wife. He was still pleased about that, but she didn't appear to share his sentiments. He wondered if her parents had somehow forced her down the aisle? He hadn't met Kendall parents, his in-laws, but he supposed that he couldn't discount that possibility. Something had clearly forced Kendall to wed him against her will.

"My makeup is ruined, isn't it?" Kendall asked, using

a shiny silver coaster as a makeshift mirror to check her face.

"You look beautiful," Michael told her. She did still look beautiful. His gaze swept over her hungrily. He wished they could skip the reception. He wished he knew if he was still welcome in her bed. "And I'm sure that the makeup artist will be available to touch you up after we get inside."

"Why are you being so nice to me?" Kendall asked, looking at him as though she didn't quite trust his behavior.

Michael smiled, he had a feeling it came across somewhat bitter, but he couldn't help it. He was hurting. "Because you're my wife," he said, unable to keep a possessive edge out of his voice.

"But," Kendall started to argue.

"It's done now, Kendall," Michael growled, conscious that the car was slowing down to a stop. He glanced out of the window, and so he missed the pained look that flashed across Kendall's face. "Smile," he muttered, as the door was thrown open for them.

Michael forced himself to smile too. He hoped that no one would be able to tell that he was faking. Months of campaigning was good practice for hiding his true feelings. It was incredibly useful now. As predicted, the makeup artist was standing by to readjust Kendall's face and hair before they walked into the reception as husband and wife. Kendall looked calmer and more settled after her hair and lipstick had been retouched. She took Michael's hand outside a gilded ballroom.

"Ladies and Gentlemen, Mr. and Mrs. Michael and Kendall Reese..." the band struck up 'Hail to the Chief' as they walked inside.

A bit premature, Michael thought, but kept the smile fixed firmly on his face as he led Kendall to a table at the front of the room.

The reception ticked by in the same strange way as the wedding ceremony. Michael was unaware of time. He was very unaware of other people too. He simply wanted to keep Kendall beside him, still half-afraid that she was going to bolt.

The room was thronging with people. There were senators, congressmen and women, governors, diplomats, Michael's old Army buddies, and celebrities. Those were the people he recognized. Tom had obviously had a hand in the guestlist. As the evening wore on, he was introduced to his mother-in-law, and to some of Kendall's friends. He in turn managed to introduce her to some of his family. He was sure that he didn't do any of the introductions justice, but he hoped people would make excuses if he seemed distracted.

They heard speeches that Michael didn't really listen to and were served food that he didn't eat, but then they were asked to lead off the dancing, and Michael couldn't help but be a little moved by the song that was chosen: *How Do I Live*, sung by Trisha Yearwood. He didn't have a clue which of the organizers had picked it out, possibly it was Kendall. He hoped that it had been, but whoever it was, they had hit the nail right on the head.

They didn't speak as they moved around the floor. It was enough for Michael just to hold her, his wife. The label still gave him a guilty thrill. She felt so right in his arms. Surely, she had to feel it too? He couldn't be imagining this connection, could he?

Kendall was looking a little more relaxed at least. Michael wasn't sure if that was due to his reassurance or to champagne on an empty stomach. He feared the latter but wasn't going to look a gift horse in the mouth. Kendall looked more like a bride, at least.

Michael was eager to leave the reception. He wanted to get Kendall away from Thomas. He wanted to get away from Thomas when it came down to it. Michael had managed to avoid being caught alone by his campaign manager so far, but he could see that Thomas was dying to talk to him, and he couldn't go on hiding from him for the rest of the night. He needed to sort things out in his own mind before he even thought about talking to the other man.

"Are you ready to go?" Michael asked Kendall at the very earliest moment that he thought leaving was feasible.

Kendall bit her lip. "Is it rude to leave now? Don't we need to stay until..."

"Until?" Michael echoed her. A smile tugged at the corner of his mouth. He raised an eyebrow at her when she couldn't answer his question.

"Well, I need to thank my mom. And Ava and Maya too."

"Your mother will pass on your thanks I'm sure," Michael said smoothly, guiding her over to the head table.

"Wait! I need to toss my bouquet!"

Michael's arched his brow in disbelief. Frankly, he hadn't thought that she would care about such traditions, especially if the wedding was something that she had been forced into.

"Well, I've never been married before," Kendall said, a hint of petulance in her voice.

And she wouldn't ever get married again, not if he had any say in the matter.

The bouquet toss caught everyone's attention, and

they were corralled into yet more pictures, so it took far longer than Michael would have liked to get away. Eventually, they managed it.

"Where are we going now?" Kendall asked as they slipped out into the hall.

"Upstairs," Michael answered, unable to entirely suppress a grin when he saw her impressed amazement.

"We have reservations?" Kendall looked surprised. "But how? Aren't I supposed to be on a plane to Europe?"

"It doesn't matter how," Michael said unwilling to hear Kendall repeat the plans that had been made for her escape. He didn't really want to go into all the 'fake' organizing that had gone into their supposedly 'fake' wedding. It was all real now and that was what he wanted Kendall to concentrate on.

Michael was just a little bit satisfied that he had managed to convince Thomas that they needed to book the Presidential suite at the hotel, even if he they never expected to get any use out of the room. It would have looked very strange if the media had discovered that he hadn't had anything arranged for the wedding night.

Michael gave his head a shake. Now he was dwelling on what should have happened today instead of what had happened.

"Is something wrong?" Kendall asked anxiously as he led her to the elevators. "I mean, apart from all... all of this?" she stumbled over the words.

Michael leant forwards and dabbed a surprise kiss against his wife's lips. "Stop looking so scared," he whispered.

"Why aren't you furious?" she whispered, looking so delightfully muddled that Michael wanted to lean towards her again, and steal a proper kiss this time. They had barely had any time alone together to talk since saying 'I do'. There was always a photographer, a family member or a political 'friend' waiting to congratulate the happy couple. Now that they were alone for an extended amount of time, the weight of the 'sham turned real' wedding started to subside.

"Do I look furious? Have I looked furious at all today?" he sighed, edging closer.

"Well, no... but."

But Michael didn't let Kendall say another word. He placed a hand gently on either side of her head and guided her lips back to his mouth. She gasped, opening herself to Michael and his talented tongue. He explored her mouth with a lazy thoroughness born from the realization that he had the rest of his life to indulge himself in learning the secrets of Kendall's body. *If* he could convince her that she wanted to stay married to him.

"Michael?"

"Kendall?" he chuckled. He would have kissed her again, but the elevator had stopped.

The air in the hallway was colder than the reception room. The change in temperature seemed to have sobered Kendall up. He hoped that a few more kisses would relax her again. He certainly wasn't planning on sleeping alone on his wedding night, no matter how the actual wedding might of come about. Fortunately, he could feel her slowly start to soften and mold herself against him.

They stopped at the door of their suite. Michael unlocked the door but made no move to go inside.

"What is it?" Kendall asked, but the end of question was punctuated by a squeal as Michael lifted her up into his arms.

"Tradition," he said casually to excuse his own sentimentality. This was something he wanted to do and if Kendall could toss her bouquet then he was certainly entitled to carry his bride over the threshold and into the room beyond.

Kendall gasped when she saw suite on the other side of the door. It was the larger than her first two apartments combined. She would have quite liked to explore the room, but Michael seemed to only have one exploration in mind, her body in the bedroom. He placed Kendall down on the huge king size bed and stared down at her with hungry eyes.

"Are we going to talk about what happened today? And where we go from here?" Kendall licked her lips uncertainly. She didn't understand what was going on. Why wasn't Michael angry? Why wasn't he yelling at her, demanding an explanation for her actions, but instead looking at her as though he was imagining her undressed?

Perhaps it wasn't such a big deal for him, Kendall wondered unhappily? He hardly held the state of marriage in particularly high regard, not judging by his first two marriages at any rate. Maybe he thought this would help his campaign even more than the jilting would have done? Maybe the divorce lawyer is already on speed dial? She didn't like the thought, but she had to consider it... maybe, just maybe, he was determined to get his use out of her while it lasted?

She was busy working out how to turn these theories around to her advantage. Clearly, Michael wasn't about to toss her out onto the street, so perhaps she would have time to demonstrate the advantages of being married to her?

Kendall was suddenly very glad for the sexy lingerie that was hidden beneath her wedding dress. She pushed herself up on her knees, reaching out a hand towards Michael. She clutched at his shirt and dragged him closer.

"You want me?" she whispered, her voice still hedged with doubt when Michael hadn't responded to her first question.

"Oh God, Kendall, if you only knew!" Michael swore, crushing their mouths together.

Kendall went weak all over. Michael was voracious as he plundered her mouth with his tongue, enacting with the slick muscle the act that Kendall knew they would be performing later with their bodies. It was enough to make her hot and achy all over.

The fear she'd been feeling all day melted away and turned into something else. She knew there would be consequences for her actions today and she knew it would probably not end well but the primal part of her could only focus on one thing. Right in this moment, Michael at least still wanted her body and was making her feel almost unbearably aroused. If her heart was going to be broken, it was going to have to wait. She wanted him naked, she wanted him inside her, and she wanted it at this very moment. Michael, however, seemed to be trying to muster some sort of an attempt at restraint.

"Slow," he whispered, speaking against Kendall's skin when she started squirming restlessly. "We have all night," Michael assured. He smoothed his hands down the sides of her dress, mapping out her figure.

"You don't have to be slow," panted Kendall impatiently. She felt Michael chuckle as he held her against his chest.

"I want to savor you," he confessed roughly, nuzzling at her neck while his large fingers fumbled with the impossibly small buttons of her wedding dress. His words made Kendall shiver. She didn't know if she had ever been savored before. It sounded rather nice. She shivered a little as the back of her dress was undone and the cool air kissed her warm skin.

"What do you want?" Michael's voice was thick with desire, but he didn't wait for an answer before he claimed her mouth again. His hands slipped beneath the delicate fabric of her wedding dress, easing it off her shoulders. "Damn," he growled, somehow instilling the word with reverence and awe as he glanced down at the ingenious creation of silk and lace that Kendall was wearing underneath her dress.

Kendall glowed under his gaze, growing breathless when she looked at his face. A man couldn't possible look at a woman like that and not want her. In fact, the glint in his eyes almost looked like something else, but no, Kendall wouldn't lose her head completely. It *couldn't* be love.

Michael bent his head, kissing the creamy swells of her breasts, while he stripped her completely of the wedding dress. "You're so beautiful," he growled, pushing her down onto the mattress. "Earlier, at the church, I thought I'd never seen anything so beautiful in my life, but now I'm not so sure if I don't prefer you like this." His voice was thick with lust and desire as his eyes raked over her body barely covered in silk and lace. It was just enough delicate fabric to appear as if she were covered but he could see the hard nub of her nipples pushing through the lace.

"Michael," Kendall gasped, hardly daring to believe what he was saying let alone trust it. She begged another kiss. At least if she kept his mouth occupied, he couldn't confuse her by making such declarations.

Michael's hands were almost more bewitching than

his words. His fingers drew nonsensical patterns over her skin, scorching her, branding her with his touch. Kendall melted into the mattress, her own fingers slipping clumsily over the buttons of Michael's shirt.

"I want you naked. I want to feel your body against mine," she mewed, tangling her fingers in his tie and whispered the words against his mouth.

"And you always get what you want?" Michael chuckled.

He was joking, Kendall thought he was joking anyway, but she tensed fearfully anyway. What if he was just toying with her before revealing how he really felt over what she had done?

"Kendall?" Michael said, stilling when he felt the sudden tension that was humming through her veins. "Baby, whatever it is, forget it? We'll figure it all out tomorrow. Tonight, let's just finally let it be about us. The real us. Whatever that is," he begged slowly, kissing the side of her neck, while his hands eased her breasts out of their cups. He fondled them tenderly, tweaking the nipples, and making it impossible for Kendall to worry about anything.

26

*W*hen Kendall woke up the next morning, someone was hammering on the hotel room door. She burrowed deep under the covers and tried to block out the noise. Michael was less inclined to ignore the disturbance.

"What the hell?" he growled, rubbing a hand over his eyes. A grumpy frown clouded his face. "If this is house-keeping then they can forget their fucking tip!" He paused in the middle of his rant to bestow a tender kiss on Kendall's lips and then he gently untangled their bodies.

Kendall watched shamelessly as Michael strolled naked across the room. He really was the most impressive specimen of a man that she had ever seen. He picked up one of the complimentary bathrobes and shrugged it on, before storming to the door and flinging it open.

"Look, I don't know-," he started angrily, but stopped short when Thomas pushed right by him and marched into the room.

Thomas's eyes swept around the suite, bulging almost out of their sockets when they caught sight of Kendall.

She held the blankets up to her chin and tried to muster a smile.

"Good morning, Thomas," Michael muttered bitterly. He gave the door a pointed glance as he imagined tossing his campaign manager back out of the room. "So?" He tightened the belt of his robe. "What can Mrs. Reese and I do for you today?"

Kendall started at hearing herself addressed as Mrs. Reese. Tom did a double take too.

"You could start by telling me what on earth happened yesterday, and what we're meant to do about it now."

"Thomas, could I speak to you privately for a moment?" Michael asked, nodding his head toward the separate sitting area of the suite. "I'm sure *my wife* would prefer not to be cross-examined while she's still in bed. I can answer your questions."

Thomas seemed both surprised and alarmed by Michael's behavior. He glanced back at Kendall, and then quickly looked away before trotting obediently into the other room.

"I won't be long," Michael said softly, turning his attention back to Kendall for a moment. "Stay just where you are," he added, a wicked gleam flashing in his eyes.

Kendall squirmed. Just the suggestion that Michael wanted her again was enough to make her body throb for his touch. She was sore and tender from the night before, but still hungry for the pleasure he bestowed.

"What are you going to tell Thomas?" she asked.

"It doesn't matter. I'll take care of it," he promised evasively, slipping out of the room and leaving Kendall on her own.

He was going to tell Thomas the truth, Michael

thought to himself, as he closed the door. He didn't know what else to do. He was just going to have to come clean with the other man.

"Well?" Thomas demanded as soon as the door was closed. He had regained a lot of his composure now that there wasn't a naked woman in the room with them. "I hope you have a good explanation. I'm certainly dying to hear it."

"No."

"No? What do you mean 'no'?"

"I mean no, I don't have a good explanation for you Tom. I don't know why Kendall came to the church yesterday. I don't know why she went through with the ceremony."

Thomas blinked at him in disbelief. "Well maybe you could tell me why *you* went through with it?"

Michael smiled sadly. "Oh, I can tell you that." He glanced back towards the other room. "I love her."

Thomas stared in horror, unable, or at least unwilling to comprehend what he was hearing. "You *love* her?" he choked, the words practically exploding from his mouth.

Michael gestured for Tom to keep his voice down.

Tom's incredulity seemed to grow by the second. "And she doesn't know?" he hissed, looking from Michael to the door and back again. "You married her. You say you love her, and she doesn't know?"

"No." Michael confessed gruffly.

"I think I need to sit down," Tom muttered, shaking his head. He sank into a nearby chair. It was a few minutes before he spoke again. "So, this means that the marriage is real?" he said slowly. "We don't have a problem on that front?" His mind was obviously in election campaign mode now. "Really, it will probably turn out better for your chances this way, although getting the sympathy vote would have been useful...Still, that wouldn't have necessarily made up for the lack of a First Lady..."

Michael cleared his throat. He wasn't sure if Tom was talking to him or merely muttering to himself. "Right. We'll have a First Lady," he said as a new and unpleasant thought occurred to him.

Maybe Kendall just wanted to be First Lady. Was that why she went through with the wedding? Michael had never thought of her as conniving. She always seemed to be above the games that other women played. He felt like she saw him as a man and not just the potential leader of the country, but he could have misjudged her. Perhaps, like everyone else, she was only interested in him because he might be President soon.

Thomas didn't notice the change in the other man's expression. "Well," he said thoughtfully, "I suppose that's something then? I assume that you want to settle things with Miss Bailey- I mean *Mrs. Reese*- on your own?"

"Yes. I'll resolve things with Kendall. All you need to know is that she is my wife and will be remaining as such for the foreseeable future."

Tom nodded. A knowing smile twitched at the edge of his lips. "Well, I'll leave the two of you alone to 'resolve things' then" he chuckled. "I think there was another way out of this suite? Give my regards to Mrs. Reese."

Once he was alone, Michael took a moment to compose himself before he returned to his wife. He was pleased to see that Kendall was still sitting in bed, looking just as delectable as when he had left her there.

"Has Thomas gone?" she asked.

"He's gone," Michael nodded, shrugging off his robe as he walked purposefully towards the bed.

"What did you say to him?" Kendall asked, but Michael was pleased to see that she was distracted by the sight of his naked, increasingly aroused body.

"Later," he growled, rejoining her in bed. "We can talk about it later."

They didn't talk about it later though. Kendall returned to the subject as they left the hotel and again in the car, but Michael always found some way to distract her. He didn't ask her to explain herself though, so she didn't try to push him for answers.

They didn't have a proper honeymoon arranged. Since they never intended to get married nothing was booked. It wasn't too suspicious. Everyone knew that Michael was busy winding up his campaign. Kendall did regret it a little though. She wanted to escape from the limelight for a while and bask in the sensation of being Michael's wife for as long as she could.

Kendall was still waiting for a shoe to drop. For the first few days after the wedding she felt a constant tension thrumming through her veins, expecting Michael to unleash on her at any moment for spoiling his plans. She had broken the rules. She had gotten too close. She had pushed things too far. It was obvious that Michael enjoyed her body and sometimes she felt like he appreciated her company as well, but that didn't mean he wanted to be forced into marriage.

He couldn't very well get rid of her before the election.

After hours of anxious contemplation, that was the only explanation that Kendall could think of that made sense. The election was only a few more days away.

Michael couldn't toss aside his brand-new wife without igniting a scandal. That was surely the only thing holding Thomas back. The campaign manager probably had the paperwork for a divorce drawn up already. Kendall had one shot at holding on to her husband. The people wanted a First Lady. That was what had gotten them into this mess. If Michael won, she had a chance. *If he lost...*

No sense borrowing trouble, Kendall told herself firmly and then pushed the worry to the back of her mind.

It was very strange going from a casual, intermittent relationship to the intensity of living in the same house. If Michael shared any of Kendall's reservations about changes- things like sharing a bathroom and seeing Kendall without her make up on- he didn't show it at all. He was sweet and accommodating, and even invited her to bring the furniture from her old house to help her feel more at home in their joint residence.

"There's not really much point in me doing that, is there?" she asked after Michael made the suggestion

"What do you mean?"

There was a strain in his voice that made Kendall look up. "Well, with any luck we won't be here for much longer. You'll be President and you'll have a brand-new home."

Or maybe "we'll" have a brand-new home? Kendall mentally willed Michael to correct her and offer some reassurance, but her hopes were unfulfilled.

"I might not get elected, Kendall."

Kendall gave Michael her full attention. "What are you talking about? Of course, you will. You have worked so hard for this."

"Yes...but, if I don't." A dark intensity filled Michael's eyes, causing Kendall to stare at him in wonder. He seemed oddly vulnerable, and she didn't think that his mood could be attributed to fears about the election.

"If you don't...?" Kendall sucked in her breath as the question she had been dreading hung silently in the air. After so many years of avoiding emotional attachment, it shocked her how much she needed him now. Michael opened his mouth to speak but seemed to think better of it. There was another long pause before he said, "Then, I'll probably need a nice long vacation."

Michael forced a smile as he spoke, trying to lighten the mood. He couldn't help noticing that he failed. Kendall wore a grim, thoughtful expression. Once again, Michael had the sense of missed opportunity as he allowed his feelings to remain unvoiced.

Kendall finally broke the uneasy silence. "It doesn't matter. You're going to win."

Michael wrapped his arms around Kendall's waist and tugged her against his chest. "Well now, you have to say that, don't you, Mrs. Reese?"

"But it's true," she insisted. "I wouldn't have come to work for you in the first place if I didn't believe that."

"No," he said thoughtfully. "I suppose you wouldn't have risked your career, would you?"

"Do you think that I'll make an okay First Lady?" Kendall asked, fishing for a clue of what her status would be after the election was over. "I mean, I'm only a speech writer. I don't really know anything about being the wife of a President."

"I think you'll make a perfect First Lady."

Kendall finally allowed herself a small smile. She

leaned her head to one side and raised an eyebrow at him. "Why?"

"I chose you too, remember?" There was a wicked gleam in Michael's eyes.

"Yes, but Michael, you chose me to-" Kendall couldn't finish that sentence because Michael captured her mouth, smothering the rest of her words beneath his lips.

"Shall I tell you why you'll be perfect?" he murmured, releasing her only once she was breathless. "Because you're sweet and beautiful. You're damn smart too. You're also-" he nibbled at her ear "-sexy as hell," he whispered.

"Oh really, and how's that going to help the country?"

"I don't know, but I know exactly how it will help the President."

$\mathcal{T}$ime passed in a blur of rallies, debates and interviews. Kendall's cheeks ached from smiling so much. She didn't dare to take a moment's rest. Election week finally arrived. As the end of the campaign loomed steadily closer and closer, the different ways that Kendall and Michael were coping became readily apparent.

Michael reminded his wife of a little boy waiting for Christmas morning who didn't know if Santa was going to bring a brand-new bike or a lump of coal. Kendall, on the other hand, was almost impossibly calm.

"We've done everything that we possibly could," she reminded Michael, the night before the election as they crawled into bed after a full day of campaigning. "Did we? I'm still not sure that we made the right call by going to Arizona last week instead of Florida," Michael argued, wriggling around uncomfortably. "Maybe if I-?"

"Enough, please! You need to get a good night's sleep tonight so that you're fresh for the morning."

"I'm never going to be able to sleep tonight," Michael

said, reaching for Kendall. His hands slid under her night-dress to give her nipples a teasing tweak. "How about you stay up and keep me company?"

"Michael," Kendall sighed, but didn't try to stop him when his hands continued wandering over her body. She hoped that a bout of lovemaking would tire Michael out enough to help him fall asleep.

It seemed to do the trick. Michael hardly managed to draw out of her body once they were both spent and sated before a soft snore bubbled out of his mouth.

Kendall nestled up against his chest, trying to fix the sensation in her mind. She was painfully conscious that today could be the end. If Michael lost the election, there was no more point to pretending that they were a *real* married couple. She didn't know how she could bear to lose him now.

She closed her eyes and snuggled closer, trying to settle her thoughts and simply enjoy her last few hours in his arms. It didn't seem like she had shut her eyes for more than a minute before the alarm clock went off. Kendall grumbled and pulled the blankets over her head, waiting for Michael to make the buzzing stop. When he didn't, she opened her eyes and was surprised to discover that he was no longer in bed.

Kendall rolled over onto her husband's side of the mattress so that she could reach the clock. She switched it off and frowned when she felt that the sheets underneath her were cool to the touch.

"Good morning, Sunshine."

Kendall spun around at the sound of her name. Michael was standing in the doorway. It was only 4:30 am, and still dark, but she could smell the cup of coffee in his hand.

"How long have you been awake?" she asked.

"Not long," Michael said sheepishly.

"You're a terrible liar. That doesn't exactly bode well for your political career."

Michael handed Kendall the coffee. "I just went for a run on the treadmill. Couldn't sleep," he shrugged. It was no wonder that he hadn't been able to sleep. Kendall could tell from the way he was anxiously shifting his weight from side to side that he was practically bouncing off the walls. "So," Michael said. "You ready to go make me a President?"

"Are *you* ready?"

"I feel like my whole life has been leading up to this day," he said, exhaling shakily. He shot a vulnerable, almost boyish smile at his wife. "Do you think that sounds stupid?"

Kendall put down her coffee and got out of bed. She walked up to Michael, wrapped her arms around his neck, and pressed a kiss against his cheek. "It doesn't sound stupid at all. You've invested so much of yourself into this campaign."

"Yeah," he murmured thoughtfully. He twined his arms around Kendall's waist and hugged her close. "Thank you for standing by me."

"There's nowhere else I wanted to be," she said earnestly.

Michael claimed her lips in a searing kiss. He hoped that Kendall remembered that sentiment. There were so many things riding on the outcome of this day. Michael was terrified by the knowledge that his marriage was one of those things. He didn't think he could lose Kendall, not now, and not ever.

"We have to get ready," he murmured, releasing

Kendall. He couldn't stand still for more than a minute. He just wanted things to start.

"Okay. I'll get dressed as soon as I finish my coffee."

Michael shot his wife a desperate look. "We can't be late," he urged, obviously taking exception to her 'time wasting'.

"We still have two hours before the polls even open," Kendall laughed, but in the end, she relented and got dressed.

They were ready by five-thirty, but Bruno wasn't due to pick them up until just before six. Michael passed the time by pacing the living room like a caged tiger.

"Please try to relax?" Kendall begged. She lifted her hands to Michael's shirt collar and straightened his tie. "Everything is going to be fine."

"You can't possibly know that."

Kendall kissed his cheek. "Well I believe it's going to be fine."

Michael looked down into her eyes, and felt a sudden, almost-overwhelming urge to tell her exactly how he felt. "Kendall," he breathed. "I lo-" but he was cut off by the chime of the doorbell.

Tom was at the front door. He had driven over with Bruno so that he could accompany Kendall and Michael to the polling booth. He talked for the entire ride, anxiously bestowing last minute advice. He seemed almost as nervous as Michael. Kendall couldn't believe that she was the calmest member of their party. She was sure it wouldn't last the whole day, but for the moment at least, she was serene and relaxed.

A mass of reporters and camera crews were waiting outside the polls when they arrived. Kendall plastered on her best "politician's wife" expression. She smiled and chatted for a few minutes after casting her ballot, laughing when one reporter asked her to tell them who she voted for. Michael gave a quick, impromptu interview, and then they climbed back into the limo again.

"Well, that's three votes I know I've got at least," Michael said.

He seemed calmer now. Kendall decided that what Michael said earlier was true. He needed to stay active to avoid obsessing about the vote.

Unhappily, the time had come for Kendall to part ways with her husband. Michael was headed to the northeast for a string of rallies, while Kendall was staying in Louisville to make a few television appearances, before heading west that afternoon to fire up the voters before the polls closed in their states.

"I'll try and give a call around lunchtime, and let you know how things are going, okay?" Michael said as the car stopped to drop him off at the airport.

"Don't worry about that. Just concentrate on the job you've got to do today, Mr. Reese."

Once things got underway, Kendall wasn't sure she ever wanted to be involved in an election campaign again. She didn't have a second to herself all day. She just smiled, waved, and tried to convince every person over the age of eighteen that crossed her path to vote for her husband. Although it was manic, there was a silver lining. She didn't have time to mope or worry about what might happen when the day was done.

By the time that Kendall climbed wearily onto the airplane that took her home to Louisville, she was no longer calm. She was a bag of nerves. Some of the results from back east had started trickling in. Things were looking okay. Michael had a tiny lead, but it was much too close to call.

Kendall had a three-and-a-half-hour flight, and she refused to let anyone tell her if the results had changed as they made the journey.

She wished that she could remain in blissful ignorance until was all over. It was stomach-churning to wait and watch every precinct report back, but she hadn't been able to avoid overhearing a news broadcast before she boarded the plane. She was determined not to listen to anything else until Michael's fate was decided.

Upon arrival in Louisville, Kendall was whisked to a waiting car.

"Can you turn that off?" she asked the driver, who was listening to the news on the radio.

He seemed puzzled but complied. She enjoyed blissful silence for the short ride downtown to the Brown Hotel where the campaign staff was waiting on returns.

At the hotel, Kendall was shown to the Presidential Suite. A bittersweet smile crossed her lips when she stepped inside, remembering the room from her wedding night.

She knew that she would have to rejoin the crowd in the ballroom eventually, so she couldn't change out of her clothes, but she kicked off her heels and turned down the lights. She helped herself to a drink from the mini bar and then sank down onto the soft bed, curling up on the luxurious mattress as she sipped her red wine. She booted up Netflix and watched the end of an old movie that she had started watching on the plane. It was hard to follow what was going on though. She was too tired and distracted to keep up with the plot.

She finished her drink and settled down on the bed more comfortably, snuggling back against the fluffy pillows. She closed her eyes, just intending to rest them. The next thing she knew, she was awakened by her phone.

Kendall fumbled in the dark for the source of the sound. The caller ID was for Maya. Was she calling to congratulate, to commiserate, or just to chat? Kendall wasn't sure she wanted to know. She let the call go to voicemail. There were two more calls that she had missed.

Was that good or bad?

Kendall thought she could hear people cheering outside, but she wasn't certain. She chewed her lip, trying to work up the courage to go downstairs and join everyone else. Before she could manage it, the door to the room flung open and Michael stepped inside.

The first thing that Kendall noticed was how tired he looked. Then she saw the serious expression on his face.

He lost.

The realization triggered a burst of panic in Kendall's chest. It took a moment to master her emotions, but then she hurried to her husband's side, feeling his disappointment keenly, but determined to console him. She threw her arms around his neck and held him tight. "I don't care what the result was. I'm so proud of you. You've worked so hard. You've done so much. I believed you were the best candidate. I still believe it, and I've never believed in anything before. We won't give up! I'll help you on a new campaign. I'll write your speeches again," she said fervently. "We'll win next time, I promise!"

Michael stared at her. His brow furrowed in confusion as he met her eyes. Then, remarkably, his lips curled up on the edges. "Well, that's good to know. I'm relieved about the speeches too. I'm going to need you in another four years."

"What?" Kendall said, confused by his smile.

Michael kissed her until she swayed in his arms. "The Associated Press just called the election. We won, baby! We won!"

"We-? I mean...you *won*?" Kendall stammered, dazed.

"You don't need to sound *quite* so surprised," Michael chuckled. He tried to drag her to his lips again, but she placed her hands on his chest and held him back. If the look on her face was anything to judge by then the meaning of his words was slowly sinking in. It had happened the same way for him. The idea was just too enormous to absorb all at once. He was going to be the President.

"Oh my God, Michael," Kendall screamed. He picked her up and twirled her around the room. "You won! I knew you could do it!"

"*We* did it," Michael corrected her firmly. "I never could have done this without you."

He bent forward to kiss her again, and this time she didn't try to stop him. Michael devoured his wife. He knew exactly how he wanted to celebrate his victory, but he also knew that they could only count on a few minutes alone. Almost on cue, the door to the suite swung open again.

"I thought I might find you up here, Michael," Tom said as he barged inside without knocking. "Good evening, Mrs. Reese," he said, acknowledging Kendall.

"Good evening, Thomas," she replied, still too dizzy with excitement to be annoyed by the interruption.

"What can we do for you, Tom?"

"You're needed downstairs. Mr. Vance is starting his concession speech. You shouldn't be missing this."

"Don't worry," Kendall said, leaning toward her husband and speaking to him in a conspiratorial whisper, "You know how much Mr. Vance likes the sound of his own voice. I'm sure we can get you back downstairs before anyone realizes you were even gone."

Kendall's prediction was correct. They arrived back in the ballroom with plenty of time to listen to the end of Mr. Vance's remarks. Then it was Michael's turn to take the floor.

"Before I say anything else, I want to thank the American people for giving me this opportunity to serve them. I want to make them a promise, that my team and I will spend the next four years proving that they made the right choice."

There was a smattering of applause here, and Michael took the opportunity to put his thoughts in order. Kendall hadn't let him prepare a speech. She was superstitiously convinced that it would jinx the election result. Michael had to speak off the cuff. Fortunately, that was something he did well. He carried on talking, finally ending with a round of thanks to his campaign team.

"...and there is of course one last person who I really need to thank, the love of my life, my wife, Kendall. She believed in me even when I didn't believe in myself. She is my constant source of inspiration and support, and is a powerful, passionate force in her own right. And before anyone asks," Michael paused for dramatic effect. "No. She didn't write this speech for me."

Laughter rippled through the crowd, while Kendall's heart gave a dangerous start. She wanted so badly to believe that Michael's words were the truth. If only she could really be the love of his life. She was convinced now that he was hers.

Michael walked straight up to her after he left the stage.

"How did I do?" he asked, smiling from ear to ear. "What was your professional opinion?"

"Well, I think you deviated from the point a little in the middle," Kendall said in a teasing tone. "But I thought that the ending was wonderful."

"Did you really? Because you know I meant it."

Kendall met his gaze. "I'm not sure that I do."

Michael swallowed hard. He had just become one of the most powerful men in the world, but now he felt vulnerable and exposed. There was only one thing standing between him and perfect happiness.

"I love you, Kendall Reese." He waited breathlessly for her reaction, bowled over in disbelief at the shock on her face.

"You love me?"

"Is it really that surprising?" Michael asked, rubbing his palm up and down her back.

Kendall nodded. "I thought you just needed me so that you could become President."

"It started that way," Michael agreed, "but then some-thing changed. I want this-" he paused to make a gesture at the room, the sweep of his arm taking in the campaign posters, ecstatic supporters and the bank of televisions declaring his win. "But I *need* you."

He stopped to stare at her. Kendall could only stare back until she noticed a frown forming on the edge of his lips. "I hoped that you felt the same way," he murmured, finally sparking her into action.

"Of course I do," she exclaimed, surprised that she

hadn't said so before. "I love you so much. That is why I kept on driving to the church. I was more afraid of losing you than anything else."

"More afraid than you were of Tom?" Michael teased, lightening the mood.

Kendall rolled her eyes and leaned against his shoulder. "You know what I mean. I just wished so hard that it could be real."

"It was real," Michael said firmly and then leaned closer to purr into her ear. "It *is* real."

Kendall tipped her lips toward her husband, inviting a deep, slow kiss, but it was not to be.

"Michael? Mrs. Reese? I need you over here."

Kendall sighed, and her husband swore under his breath, as Tom interrupted them again.

"I think I'm going to make him ambassador to Fiji," Michael muttered.

Kendall's lips spread into a grin. "Mr. President, that's an *excellent* idea."

THE END

FROM AVERY

I hope that you enjoyed reading, *His First Lady*. If you did, please consider leaving a review. Your recommendations help other readers find my stories. Plus, hearing directly from readers about what works (or doesn't!) helps me know what to write next.

Would you like to read more of Michael and Kendall's story? Do you wonder what happened after the election?

If so, check out my website, www.averyscott.com where you can read outtakes and extra scenes from all my books (including Michael and Kendall's trip to the kennel to pick out a First Dog!)

On the site, you can also join my mailing list to hear about new releases, like **Too Hot to Handle**, coming Summer 2019.

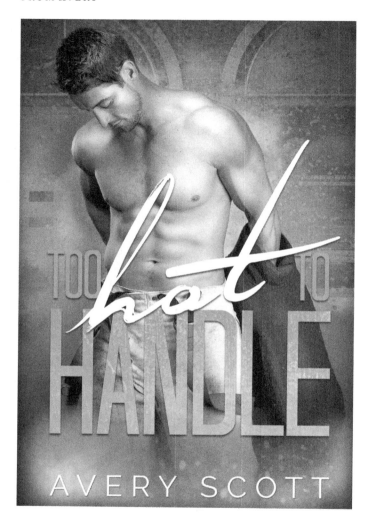

Made in the USA
Columbia, SC
28 February 2019